THE CLUE IN THE JEWEL BOX

An antique dealer's revelation about a former queen's priceless heirloom starts Nancy on a trail of exciting adventures.

Madame Alexandra, now living incognito in River Heights, asks Nancy to find her missing grandson. With only one clue to go on—a faded photograph of the prince at the age of four—the young detective begins her search, which rapidly involves her in a series of dangerous and harrowing adventures. When Nancy needs help, she calls on Bess, George, Burt, Dave, and her special friend, Ned. How Nancy's discovery of the heirloom's secret unmasks a slick imposter and reunites the long-separated family climaxes this suspense-filled mystery story.

"Ned, there's a pickpocket!" Nancy exclaimed

NANCY DREW MYSTERY STORIES

The Clue in the Jewel Box

BY CAROLYN KEENE

PUBLISHERS *Grosset & Dunlap* NEW YORK

A NATIONAL GENERAL COMPANY

PUBLISHED SIMULTANEOUSLY IN CANADA

LIBRARY OF CONGRESS CATALOG CARD
NUMBER: 72-77109
ISBN: 0-448-09520-3 (TRADE EDITION)
ISBN: 0-448-19520-8 (LIBRARY EDITION)

PRINTED IN THE UNITED STATES OF AMERICA

Contents

CHAPTER I

A Stolen Wallet

"No, a silver pen isn't exactly what I'm looking for," Nancy Drew explained to the jewelry salesman in the department store.

The slim, attractive girl with lovely reddish-blond hair waited while he reached beneath the counter to get another item.

"Here's something perfect," he declared. "This handsome jewelry box is very new. It's a clever reproduction of one owned by a ruler in Europe two centuries ago."

Nancy was disappointed to learn that it was a reproduction. She had hoped to find something original and unusual for her father's birthday.

"It's lovely," she said, "but—"

"The original box has a strange history," the salesman went on. Knowing of Nancy's reputation as an amateur detective, he hoped to capture her interest with hints of mystery. "Its first owner was a king disliked by his subjects. One night he was spirited away, and—"

Before he could finish the romantic tale, he was interrupted by a woman customer who was tapping on the glass counter for attention.

"I'd better not make a hasty decision," Nancy said politely to the man. "Thank you very much."

She walked off and took an elevator that would take her to the restaurant floor. Nancy thought, "That jewelry box certainly looked genuine. Maybe Dad would like it for his birthday after all."

She was going to have luncheon with Bess Marvin and George Fayne, who were cousins and Nancy's closest friends. The girls had not arrived, so Nancy sat down in the lounge to wait for them.

"Oh dear!" murmured a voice nearby.

Turning her head, Nancy saw that the chair beside her was occupied by an attractive, elderly woman in a dark-blue dress. The pallor of her creamy skin held the girl's attention. Obviously the woman was ill.

"Can I help you?" Nancy asked quickly.

The woman fumbled in a purse, then shakily handed her a card. It bore the name Marie Alexandra, and an address, 14 Downey Street.

"Please take me to my home," she whispered with a slight foreign accent.

Before Nancy could reply, Bess and George entered the lounge. When she told them about

"Can I help you?" Nancy asked

the woman's request, both declared that they would postpone their luncheon.

"We'll go with you to Mrs. Alexandra's," Bess said.

"Do you have your car, Nancy?" George asked.

"No, it's at the service station. We'll have to take a taxi."

Nancy assisted the woman to her feet very gently, and was rewarded with a grateful smile.

The three girls made slow progress to the street. They summoned a taxi and helped Mrs. Alexandra step into it. Nancy gave the Downey Street address to the driver.

"Thank you—thank you," the panting woman murmured, and slumped back in a faint.

The girls chafed Mrs. Alexandra's hands and fanned her. Her pocketbook had fallen to the floor and several articles had tumbled out. One of these was a jeweled, monogrammed bottle of smelling salts, which Bess opened and held under the woman's nostrils.

"She's coming to now," Bess said a moment later as the woman's eyelids fluttered.

Relieved, Nancy reached down to pick up the handbag and its scattered contents. Almost at her feet lay a gold-framed miniature photograph of a little boy in a sailor suit. He was about four years old. She stared at the quaint picture, then turned it over. The back of the case was glass. Underneath were several locks of hair, secured with tiny ruby clasps.

"This is very unusual," Nancy thought.

She had no opportunity to show the miniature to Bess or George. As the taxi drew up in front of a medium-sized house, she replaced all the articles in the handbag and turned to assist Mrs. Alexandra.

"Can you walk if we help you?" she inquired.

"Yes, I think so," the woman answered softly.

Bess and George supported her on either side, while Nancy paid the taxi driver and darted ahead to ring the doorbell. The door was opened by a maid in a spotless white uniform.

"Oh!" the woman cried when she saw her mistress being half-carried. "Madame Marie!"

She opened the door wide and pointed to a brocade-covered couch in the living room. The girls led the woman to it.

"Shall we call a doctor?" George inquired.

"No, that will not be necessary. These spells do not last very long," Mrs. Alexandra answered. "Anna will take care of me."

The maid seemed unusually capable in attending her mistress. With loving hands she made the woman comfortable and gave her hot tea which quickly revived her.

All this time Nancy had been silently admiring the luxurious furnishings of the room. On the walls hung elegant tapestries. Beautiful pieces of furniture were upholstered with hand-embroidered silks. Rare objects of glass and porcelain stood on a table and a desk.

One piece in a curio cabinet captured Nancy's interest. It was a pink enamel Easter egg poised on a tiny gold pedestal. Its rounded top was encrusted with delicate gold work.

"I've never seen anything like it," Bess whispered in awe.

Hearing the comment, Mrs. Alexandra raised herself to a sitting position. She remarked that the Easter egg had been brought from abroad.

Turning to her maid, she said, "Anna, I must talk to these girls who have been so kind."

The words, quietly spoken, were regarded by the maid as an order to leave the room. Graciously Mrs. Alexandra thanked Nancy and her friends for their help, then carefully wrote their names in an attractive little address book.

Observing their interest in the art objects, she pointed out several which were inside a curio cabinet. Among these was a silver box that looked very much like the one at the jewelry counter in the department store. Nancy wondered if this might be the original. She spoke of her search for a distinctive birthday gift for her father.

"Of course I never could afford anything so rare as these lovely pieces." She sighed.

"You might be surprised." Mrs. Alexandra

smiled rather mysteriously. "Why not go to Mr. Faber, who is an antique dealer? Mention that I sent you. I think he will be able to help you."

She summoned Anna and asked for one of the antique dealer's business cards. On it she wrote a message in a foreign language unfamiliar to Nancy. Realizing that Mrs. Alexandra was becoming tired, the girls now said good-by.

"Wasn't it exciting?" Bess asked when they reached the street. "And didn't you just love Mrs. Alexandra? She's so charming."

"And her treasures are exquisite," Nancy said. "I was especially impressed with the Easter egg."

"Right now I'll take my eggs in omelet form without gold trimmings," said Bess, giggling.

"Oh, that appetite of yours!" Nancy teased.

The girls walked back to the center of River Heights' business section, then turned in to Water Street.

They were halfway down the block when a wiry built man darted from an alleyway and brushed past the girls. He glanced back anxiously, then quickly entered a shabby-looking apartment house.

"That fellow acts as if he were running away from someone," Nancy remarked, turning around. "Look! A crowd has gathered at the corner!"

Retracing their steps, the girls joined the excited group. In the center of the circle stood a young man, angrily accusing a second young man of having picked his pocket.

The other defended himself. "I was walking along the street, minding my own business, when you grabbed me! I never saw your wallet!"

The argument waxed warmer, and a police officer arrived. Nancy edged closer.

"Excuse me," she said. "I saw a young man who looks like this brown-haired one. He was running up the street and had on the same color suit."

"There!" cried the alleged culprit triumphantly. "I've been mistaken for the real thief!"

"Which way did the fellow go?" the officer asked.

She directed him to the four-story apartment building, and he hurried off. Everyone followed.

Scarcely had the policeman entered the building when a figure appeared on a fire escape above an alley. Light as a cat, the man leaped to the ground and fled.

"That's the one!" cried Nancy.

The heavy-set officer came back and ran after the thief, commanding him to halt. Instead, the young man squeezed through a gap between two buildings and vanished.

"Look!" Nancy cried. "He dropped the wallet!"

Had he deliberately thrown it away? the young detective wondered. A moment later the policeman returned.

"Sorry I couldn't overtake that guy," he said, handing the wallet to its owner. "I'll make a report to headquarters. Name, please?"

"Francis Baum," the other replied, checking the contents. "Never mind the report. I'm satisfied to get my stuff back."

He examined the contents carefully. Nancy, who stood close beside him, saw part of a business card. Her photographic mind noted:

thson
ter St.

"My money is all here," the owner assured the policeman. "Thanks for your trouble."

Francis Baum and the man he had accused walked off, and the crowd dispersed. Bess and George would have gone on also, but Nancy held them back.

"Just a minute," she said. "I want to search the ground between those two buildings."

"Surely you don't think the thief is still there!" George protested, following reluctantly.

"No, but I thought I saw something fall from the wallet when it was dropped."

"The policeman would have found it," Bess argued. "If we're ever to eat—"

"Here is something against the wall!" Nancy interrupted excitedly and stooped to pick it up. She held up the slightly soiled photograph of a small boy wearing a sailor suit.

"This is the same child whose picture was in

Mrs. Alexandra's miniature!" she cried. "Do you suppose she's related to Francis Baum?"

"Haven't the slightest idea," Bess replied, shrugging her shoulders. "And look! There's a hamburger stand. George and I have an appointment at three o'clock, so we ought to eat."

"Please do," Nancy said. "I want to go to Faber's first."

The young detective went on alone to the antique shop. It was an inconspicuous place on a busy street. A bell jingled as she entered.

A pleasant-faced man emerged from a rear workroom. Nancy explained that she was trying to find a gift for her father, and handed him the business card with Mrs. Alexandra's message on it.

"Oh, Madame sent you herself." The shop owner beamed, speaking with a noticeable accent. "Ah yes, I am honored to serve you."

The little man moved briskly about the cluttered room, scanning various objects.

"No, I have nothing suitable now," he finally said. "You must give me a few days."

Before leaving the shop, Nancy decided to show him the photograph she had found. She inquired if he knew who the boy might be.

With trembling hands Mr. Faber took the picture of the child in the sailor suit.

"Where did you get this?" he asked tensely. "Tell me! Tell me at once!"

CHAPTER II

After a Suspect

Astonished by the tone of Mr. Faber's voice and his interest in the photograph, Nancy readily told how it had come into her possession.

"Unbelievable!" the antique dealer murmured. "You say this picture belongs to a young man named Francis Baum?"

"I'm pretty sure it fell from his wallet," Nancy replied.

"Please describe him," the shop owner pleaded. "Did Francis Baum bear any resemblance to this boy in the photograph?"

"Why, no. Mr. Baum is tall and has a dark complexion. The boy is very fair."

"The age of Francis Baum?" he asked quickly.

"Well, it's difficult to say. He might be in his late twenties—or possibly a little younger," Nancy replied.

Nancy's curiosity had grown steadily as Mr.

Faber queried her. She longed to ask a few questions of her own, but wisely waited.

"You wonder perhaps why I ask you so much," he said. "The answers concern the happiness of Madame Alexandra, a royal lady indeed. You see, the boy in this photograph is her long-lost grandson!"

"Please tell me more," Nancy urged.

"Years ago, when revolution came to their country, the little boy was taken away secretly by his nurse. His mother, father, sisters, the entire family—except the grandmother—perished at the hands of the enemy."

"How dreadful!" Nancy murmured.

"Those were terrifying years," the antique dealer went on sadly. "Madame Alexandra, through the aid of loyal friends, escaped. Since then she has devoted herself to a search for her grandson."

"The nurse has never been traced?"

"It is believed that she came to America, but here the trail ends. If the grandson still lives, he must be thirty years old. You understand now how important it is that we find Francis Baum?"

"Indeed I do," Nancy replied. "I'll gladly help you trace him."

Nancy had inherited her love of mystery. She was the daughter of Carson Drew, a well-known lawyer, who often handled criminal cases. Her mother had died when she was three, and since then the Drews' home in River Heights had been managed for her and her father by capable Hannah Gruen.

Nancy's first case was *The Secret of the Old Clock,* and her recent one, *The Quest of the Missing Map.*

"Will Francis Baum be difficult to find?" the man questioned her anxiously.

"He shouldn't be," Nancy assured him. "No doubt he's listed in the phone book."

Acting upon the suggestion, Mr. Faber called to an assistant in the back room. He asked that the book be brought to him at once. Ivan, a young man with a pleasant grin, appeared with the directory. Unfortunately Baum's name was not listed in it.

"I'll trace him somehow," Nancy assured the dealer. "The policeman who recovered the stolen wallet must have his address."

"If you find Francis Baum, I will reward you richly for the sake of my friend Madame Alexandra," the shopkeeper declared.

"Oh, I don't want a reward," Nancy protested with a laugh. "I'll find him just for the fun of it, and to help Mrs. Alexandra."

"But I will repay you in some way," the man insisted. "Maybe by obtaining a handsome gift for your father. A gentleman's box perhaps?"

"I'm sure he would like one."

"That kind of box is something very special,"

said Ivan, grinning at Nancy. "In Europe my boss's father and grandfather were famous jewelers who made many pieces for royal families.

"Mr. Faber's father once constructed a little train for a prince," Ivan went on. "The locomotive was of platinum, and the cars were gold. It ran, too."

"Was Mrs. Alexandra's Easter egg made by your father?" Nancy asked.

"Ah, so you have seen it!" he commented.

"Only the outside."

"Madame Alexandra's Easter egg was indeed made by my famous father," Mr. Faber declared. "It contains a most unusual object. You must ask her to disclose the secret."

"I really don't know her well enough to do that," Nancy replied.

"If you find her grandson, no favor will be too great to ask." The shop owner smiled. "Yes, you must see the wonderful contents of her Easter egg. The gift was presented to her by her son, the king."

"A king?" Nancy repeated in bewilderment. "Then Mrs. Alexandra—"

Mr. Faber looked a bit dismayed. "You did not know?"

"I had no idea."

"Madame Alexandra prefers that no special deference be shown her," Mr. Faber explained. "She does not mind if a few discreet people know who she is, but if her true identity became known to everyone, she would be subjected to the kind of publicity she wishes to avoid."

"I understand. I'll do everything I can to help her," Nancy promised.

A few minutes later she left the shop, still excited by the amazing story Mr. Faber had told her. She went directly to police headquarters.

To her disappointment, no record had been made of Francis Baum's address because he had got his wallet back immediately after it had been stolen. Chief McGinnis said he would instruct the officer who had seen Baum to be on watch for him.

Throughout the afternoon she searched diligently for the mysterious stranger, making many inquiries. At length, weariness and hunger forced her into a snack shop not far from the river docks.

"Finding Francis Baum isn't going to be as easy as I thought," she reflected, biting into a toasted cheese sandwich.

Through a window Nancy absently watched a ferryboat tie up at the dock. Passengers alighted, and others boarded the vessel.

Suddenly her gaze was drawn to a young man who looked familiar. The thief who had snatched Francis Baum's wallet!

Nancy quickly paid her check and left the shop. As she gazed down the street, the young detective saw the man board the ferry.

"There he goes!" she thought excitedly, then reflected, "Or is he the man who was mistaken for the thief?"

Before Nancy could decide whether or not to follow him, the boat's whistle warned her that the ferry was about to leave. There was no time to think further—the man would escape if she did not act instantly.

Running as fast as she could, Nancy reached the dock a moment before the gate closed. She hurriedly bought a ticket, then dashed aboard the crowded deck. The ropes were cast off and the vessel edged away.

The young detective gazed about in search of her quarry. To her annoyance he was not in sight.

"But he's aboard," Nancy said to herself.

She looked at the indoor lunch counter, but there was no sign of the pickpocket. Disappointed, she returned to the deck.

During the past few minutes there had been a sudden change in the weather. Now Nancy was nearly blown off her feet by a strong gust of wind.

As the boat churned through the choppy waves, Nancy scanned the clouds. They were black. She began to shiver in her thin sleeveless dress.

A few moments later, however, the young detective completely forgot her discomfort. She had caught a glimpse of the suspect near the port railing!

Before she could reach the man, a huge wave

struck the ferryboat. Passengers were thrown off balance. Several women screamed.

The next instant there was a blinding flash of lightning, followed by a heavy roll of thunder. Rain came down in a torrent, blotting out all view of the river.

Gasping, Nancy tried to find shelter in the cabin, but others ahead of her jammed the passageway. In the milling throng she could no longer see the man she was following.

Suddenly, from off the port bow, came the deep-throated whistle of an oncoming boat. The ferry swerved sharply to avoid a collision, but not in time.

There was a terrific impact as the two craft crashed into each other. Flung sideways, Nancy went rolling down the tilted deck.

CHAPTER III

A Lost Formula

STRUGGLING to her feet, Nancy grasped the railing for support. Children were crying. Men and women were yelling as passengers trapped in the cabin fought to escape.

"Keep cool!" shouted a deck hand, trying to avert a panic. "We'll reach the dock safely."

Nancy repeated his message to those about her. She helped people to their feet, and tried to comfort the children.

When it was evident that the vessel had not been damaged below the water line, the passengers calmed down. But they jammed the decks while the crippled boat glided slowly toward River Heights.

Recalling why she had come aboard, Nancy gazed about, searching once more for the suspected thief. She decided it was hopeless to locate him in the crowd. But just as the ferryboat grated against the dock, she saw him.

He was standing close to a man whose right leg had been injured. To her disgust, the suspect stealthily reached his hand into the other's coat pocket and removed a billfold. Now she was convinced he was the man who had stolen Francis Baum's wallet.

"Stop thief!" Nancy shouted, but amid the commotion her warning went unheeded.

She tried to force her way forward, but the crowd kept her from moving more than a few feet. By now the boat was ready to discharge passengers. The thief was the first to disembark.

By the time she reached the dock, he had vanished. Nancy was dismayed. "But at least I can supply the police with an accurate description of the pickpocket," she thought. "He's about thirty, medium height, has brown hair, and walks with short, quick steps."

She saw an officer and told him about the pickpocket. He wrote everything in his report book and thanked her.

It was still raining, so Nancy took a taxi home. She rang the bell at the side door. Mrs. Gruen, middle-aged and kindly, opened the door and gasped at the girl's appearance.

"Nancy, where have you been?" she asked. "Will you never learn to carry an umbrella?"

"Never." The young detective laughed, kicking off her water-soaked shoes on the cellar stairway landing.

"Did you have a good lunch?" the housekeeper asked.

"No, just a sandwich," Nancy replied. "But please don't worry about that. It must be nearly dinnertime."

"It is," Mrs. Gruen said. "And if I am not mistaken, there's your father now."

A car had turned into the driveway. Nancy hurried to her room, changed into dry clothes, and ran down the stairs to greet him.

"Why, Dad!" she exclaimed. "What's wrong? You look mad enough to eat someone."

"I've lost an extra wallet I was carrying," Mr. Drew said shortly. "I'm afraid it was stolen."

"Stolen! How did it happen?" Nancy asked.

"I'm not absolutely certain. I didn't miss it until an hour ago."

"You didn't lose much money, I hope."

"A good bit—not to mention several important notations. The money wasn't mine," Mr. Drew explained. "It was a donation to the River Heights Boys Club."

"That's a shame. Perhaps you dropped the wallet, and it will be returned," Nancy suggested.

"I'm sure it was stolen. In fact, I recall that at noon, when I stood in line at a cafeteria, a man directly behind kept brushing against me."

"What did he look like, Dad?"

"I didn't take particular notice. A fellow of medium height with brown hair."

"Did he walk with short, quick steps?"

"Yes," Mr. Drew replied. "He got out of line and hurried off. Why all these questions?"

His daughter related her experiences of the day. Mr. Drew agreed that probably the pickpocket was the same man who had taken his extra wallet.

"Dad, I'll recognize that thief if ever I see him again," Nancy concluded. "Would you like me to capture him for you?"

"Indeed I would," her father replied grimly. "But let's think about something nicer—the picnic, for instance."

"What picnic?" Nancy inquired in surprise.

"Didn't I tell you? Some of my associates have arranged a father-daughter outing at Walden Park. We're a little bit late. I phoned Hannah. She'll have everything ready for us."

In the kitchen Nancy found the housekeeper tucking a Thermos into a well-filled food hamper.

"I can't wait to dig into this," Nancy said as she glanced over the contents.

Fortunately the late-afternoon sun was drying the ground quickly. Mr. Drew's good humor returned as he walked with Nancy to the park. Upon arriving, they found a group of River Heights lawyers and their daughters.

The Drews were given an enthusiastic welcome but teased about being late. When the men heard the story of the stolen wallet, they became concerned.

"During the past two weeks," declared one of them, "River Heights has had an alarming increase in petty thievery. It's time something was done."

"You're right," Mr. Drew agreed. "Well, my daughter says she's going to catch the pickpocket who took my wallet."

"And she probably will," said Ida Trevor, who greatly admired the young detective.

Nancy smiled, then said, "At any rate, I'd like to get back the money for the Boys Club."

Following the picnic supper, there were games of competition for the fathers and their daughters. Victory crowned the efforts of the Drews in several contests.

They lost a short race, however, to Judge and Marian Howells. As the Howells crossed the finish line, a compact that the judge was keeping for his daughter fell from his pocket. The enamel cover broke in half.

"There, I've done it!" the man exclaimed. "Why can't our girls have pockets large enough for their beauty gadgets?"

"What we need is an enamel which is noncrackable," said Mr. Drew.

The judge replied, "Many years ago such an enamel was developed. But unfortunately the process is not known today."

Launching into the history of various enamel processes, he told of its early use by the Egyptians, Babylonians, and Romans.

"There was a revival of the art in the nineteenth century, and beautiful, unbreakable pieces were made. But that method has been lost, too."

"Do you suppose it will ever be recovered?" Nancy asked.

"Oh, it may turn up sometime," the judge said, "and bring its finder great riches."

Nancy enjoyed the picnic and was sorry when it ended. But the adventures of the day had given her much to mull over before she fell asleep. After church services the following day, her thoughts once more turned to the lost prince and the secret in the Easter egg.

At breakfast Monday morning, while Nancy was sipping orange juice, the mail arrived. One letter was addressed to Nancy. Mrs. Alexandra's name was in the upper left-hand corner. With mounting interest Nancy opened it.

"Oh, Hannah, what an unexpected surprise! I'm invited to tea at four this afternoon at Mrs. Alexandra's!" she cried. "Bess and George too!"

"That's nice," the housekeeper said absently.

"It will be exciting, I'm sure! Mrs. Alexandra may show us the contents of her wonderful Easter egg!"

Enthusiastically Nancy ran to telephone George and Bess. A lengthy discussion of what to wear followed and how to act in the presence of royalty.

"I suggest," Mrs. Gruen advised, overhearing the conversation, "that you just act naturally."

Exactly at four o'clock the invited guests presented themselves at Mrs. Alexandra's home. Because they now knew of their hostess's intriguing background, Bess and George felt less at ease than on their first meeting. But they soon relaxed because Mrs. Alexandra was most gracious.

"I am glad that you went to see Mr. Faber, Nancy," she said, smiling. "He told me on the telephone you had been there.

"Mr. Faber also said that unwittingly he had revealed my identity to you," the woman went on. "I beg of you girls not to mention this to anyone. I came to your lovely town to avoid publicity."

"Is that why no one addresses you as Your Majesty, Mrs. Alexandra?" asked Bess. "It's customary, isn't it?"

"In my country, yes," the former queen replied. "When I came to your shores, I decided to adopt the customs here. So now I am Mrs. Alexandra. But Anna cannot accept this. We compromised." Lines of amusement showed around the corners of the royal lady's mouth. "Now Anna addresses me as Madame Marie."

With the arrival of tea, Nancy and her friends tried not to stare at the handsome silver service which Anna placed before her mistress. Engraved on one side of the teapot was a pheasant, while on the other was a monogram, combined with a golden royal crown.

To the amazement of the girls, Anna washed each cup and saucer in a silver basin, then carefully dried the lovely china pieces with a dainty lace-bordered linen towel before handing them to her mistress.

"An Old World custom," Mrs. Alexandra explained, her eyes twinkling. "The towel Anna uses was hand-loomed by a dear friend. You see it has my initials with the royal insignia above it."

As the girls sipped tea and ate delicious little cakes, their hostess chatted about her art treasures. She seemed particularly fond of a beautiful gold-and-blue tapestry showing a gay ballet scene.

"This piece was woven especially for me when I resided in the palace," she told the girls. "I value it almost as highly as the Easter egg."

Nancy's gaze went swiftly to the cabinet where the exquisite little ornament stood on its gold pedestal. She longed to learn its secret, yet hesitated to make the request.

"Anna, please bring the Easter egg to me," Mrs. Alexandra requested, almost as if she had read Nancy's thoughts.

The servant removed the object from the curio cabinet, then carefully placed it on a mahogany table in front of her mistress.

"Now I shall show you a truly remarkable treasure," Mrs. Alexandra said softly.

CHAPTER IV

Royal Treasures

As Nancy, Bess, and George waited expectantly, Mrs. Alexandra raised the lid of the enamel Easter egg. Rising from a nest of velvet was a tiny tree made of emeralds. A delicately fashioned golden nightingale was perched on a branch.

"How lovely!" Bess exclaimed in awe.

Mrs. Alexandra pressed a concealed spring and the nightingale began to sing. The song was brief and somewhat artificial, but nevertheless amazing. Nancy thought she detected words and repeated them to herself. Then she decided she must be mistaken since Mrs. Alexandra did not mention them. The former queen said, "I treasure this bird not only for itself, but because it was given to me by my son. It was only a short time before his untimely death," she added. "It is my hope that someday I will find my grandson and pass it on to him. Michael would be nearly thirty years old now."

Nancy had not intended to tell the story of Francis Baum, fearing that it might prove to be another disappointment to the former queen. Shortly, however, Mrs. Alexandra revealed that Michael's nurse had had a photograph of the boy identical to the miniature she possessed. Excitedly Nancy told about meeting with the young man and the picture she had found.

"Perhaps he is my grandson!" the woman declared in an agitated voice. "Tell me, did he resemble the boy in the photograph?"

Nancy was compelled to reply that she had noticed no similarity.

"Please find him!" Mrs. Alexandra urged. "Even if he is not Michael, he may know what has become of him." Nancy promised to do everything possible to trace the missing prince.

After the girls had left the house, Bess remarked, "I feel as if I had been dreaming. What did you think of the Easter egg, Nancy?"

"It's beautiful," she replied. "But to tell the truth, I was a bit disappointed. The nightingale didn't sing as it should have."

"I noticed the same thing!" George agreed. "It didn't even sound like a bird."

Nancy returned thoughtfully, "Oh, well, the work was perfect otherwise. Who are we to criticize royal treasure?" She laughed. "My job is to find Francis Baum."

Upon reaching home Nancy wrote down the

incomplete name and address which she had glimpsed on the card in the young man's wallet. Curiously she stared at the letters:

thson
ter St.

"If I can only fill these out, I may be able to contact someone who knows Mr. Baum."

Nancy pored over the telephone directory, eliminating name after name. Finally she came to one that seemed to be a good possibility—J. J. Smithson, 25 Oster Street.

"That might be worth investigating."

The next afternoon she walked with Bess and George to Oster Street in the business section.

J. J. Smithson proved to be the owner of a small leather-goods shop. He readily answered Nancy's questions. Francis Baum had worked for him only a few days. "He didn't like this kind of work," the man said. "I haven't seen Baum since the day he quit, but I believe he still lives at Mrs. Kent's guesthouse nearby."

Nancy obtained the address, and the girls continued on. Mrs. Kent, the landlady, repeated Francis Baum's name, then shook her head.

"He was here," she said, "but moved out."

"Did he leave a forwarding address?" Nancy asked.

"No, he didn't. I'll tell you how you might trace him, though. He sends his laundry to the Eagle Home Service."

"Isn't that across the river?" Nancy inquired.

"Yes, it is—a long distance from here."

The girls thanked Mrs. Kent for the information, then discussed what they should do.

"Let's go by ferryboat tomorrow," Bess suggested, and the others agreed.

On the way home Nancy chose a route past the old apartment building where the pickpocket had nearly been caught.

"You don't expect him to be here!" Bess gasped.

"It won't hurt to look," Nancy replied.

Windows on the lower floor were wide open. As the girls slowly passed one of them, they heard angry voices coming from inside.

"You can't hide here!" a man shouted.

"Sounds like an argument," said George.

"You know the police may be watching this place!" the man cried out. "You're not going to get me into trouble! Clear out!"

"I have a hunch the pickpocket is hiding in there," Nancy whispered.

The argument grew hotter, but suddenly the window was slammed down and the girls could hear no more.

At once Nancy turned to her friends. "George, you and Bess get a policeman! I'll go into the apartment house and see what I can find out."

"Please be careful," Bess warned her friend.

The instant the girls had gone, Nancy entered the building. The outer lobby was deserted. Finding the inner door unlocked, she went into the hallway.

"I wonder which apartment the men are in," she mused, tiptoeing down the hallway.

Suddenly a door a little distance away from her opened. A man rushed out, slamming it behind him.

He resembled the pickpocket!

Nancy wanted a closer look at him and gazed about for a place to observe him unnoticed. Near her was a telephone booth. She darted inside.

"If he *is* the pickpocket, I'll follow him!" she decided.

Unfortunately the man spotted Nancy and recognized her. Angrily he ran toward her.

"This *is* the pickpocket," she concluded. "He saw me and knows I heard what was said!"

Fearful that the man meant to harm her, Nancy slammed shut the glass-paneled door of the booth. To her consternation he took a piece of wood from his pocket and wedged it under the crack.

"There! How do you like that?" the pickpocket sneered. He dashed back to the room, opened the door, and shouted a warning to someone inside. Then he ran from the building.

Meanwhile, Nancy pushed with all her strength against the door, but it would not move. The wedge held fast. She was trapped!

Instinctively she searched her purse for a coin to deposit in the telephone and get help, but had none. Thoroughly alarmed, Nancy pounded on the door, but her cries went unheard.

"Oh dear! That pickpocket will be blocks away before I get out of here!" she thought.

The wedge beneath the door could not be moved, even when she pried at it with a nail file. The bit of steel broke in her hand.

Nancy's frustration changed to desperation. "I'll smash the glass with the heel of my shoe!"

Fortunately at that moment Bess and George arrived with a policeman. Nancy's shouts drew their attention.

"The thief escaped!" she gasped as the officer jerked open the door. "He locked me in here, and then ran out the front door."

"Front door? Why, when we were up the street," said George, "we saw a man climb through one of the windows. Officer Kelly chased him, but he had too big a start."

"That must have been the pickpocket's pal in the apartment," Nancy replied, adding, "When the thief warned him about me, he escaped through the window so I couldn't identify him later."

"Which door did the fellow you saw come out of?" Officer Kelly asked.

Nancy pointed. "I think it was the third one."

The officer rapped sharply on it. For several seconds there was no answer. Then the door opened a crack. A woman peered into the hall.

"What do you want?" she asked, frightened.

The policeman walked into the untidy room.

"There's no one here except me," the woman whined. "Who are you after?"

"A pickpocket who hid in this building."

"Not in my rooms," the woman maintained.

"Didn't someone jump from a window here?"

"No!"

"Do you live alone?" the officer inquired.

"Well, no, I got a husband," the woman answered. "He has a cousin who sticks around here sometimes when he's in trouble."

"Trouble?"

"Cordova has a way of gettin' mixed up in things," the woman answered with a shrug. "But I ain't sayin' it's dishonest."

"This man Cordova—" Nancy put in, "he's about thirty, isn't he, medium height and walks with short, quick steps?"

"Yeah, that sounds like him," the woman muttered.

Officer Kelly asked a few additional questions before leaving, but he could not get an admission from her that either the husband or the cousin had been there a few minutes before.

"I'll check up on her," the policeman promised as he said good-by to Nancy and her friends. "We'll watch this building and try to catch that pickpocket."

Shortly afterward, Nancy left Bess and George

at the library, then decided to stop at Mr. Faber's shop. She was nearly there when she met her father.

"Fancy meeting you here!" she said, grinning.

"I've been interviewing a client in this neighborhood," Mr. Drew told her.

"Have you a free moment, Dad?" Nancy asked.

"Sure do. I'm between appointments." He smiled affectionately.

"Then I have an idea!" Nancy cried, her gaze roving to the creaking business sign which bore Faber's name. "You must see this shop." To herself she added, "Maybe I can find out what Dad would like for a birthday present."

"I'm not going to buy anything!" insisted the lawyer.

Giving Mr. Drew no opportunity to protest further, his daughter steered him inside. Mr. Faber seemed genuinely pleased to meet the lawyer, and at a wink from Nancy immediately asked about his likes and dislikes in art objects.

"Oh, anything goes with me," Mr. Drew replied pleasantly. "But I'd like to look around."

The little man beamed. As Mr. Drew moved off to view the collection in the cluttered shop, Mr. Faber whispered to Nancy, "A gentleman's box would be exactly right for your distinguished-looking father.

"In ancient times a gentleman was known by the personal chest he carried when traveling," the dealer went on, warming to his subject. "A lady was judged by her jewel box. Jewels always have been a convenient kind of wealth to carry—far easier than money. Rulers forced to flee from their countries in time of war usually saved part of their fortunes that way."

"And sold them to get money?" Nancy asked.

"Exactly."

"Speaking of jewels," said Nancy, "how could Mrs. Alexandra bring so many valuables with her when she fled from her country?"

"Madame is a very clever woman," the shop owner replied. "She carried a small fortune secreted in a jewel box. It was so unique that it deceived everyone. Her only other possession was the handsome Easter egg case."

"But I saw so many lovely things in her home," Nancy declared as her father rejoined them.

"All those treasures were recovered after Mrs. Alexandra reached America. For years I was busy locating her family possessions around the world. She wanted them so badly that she sold many of her jewels to obtain them."

"How was she able to leave Europe?" Nancy inquired. "Did she wear a disguise when she crossed the border from her country?"

"She dressed as a peasant woman," Mr. Faber explained. "That was why the soldiers were not suspicious when they examined the Easter egg and the jewel box. They didn't open them. The men assumed that both objects were copies of real pieces."

"You say Mrs. Alexandra was able to save a fortune?" Mr. Drew's curiosity was aroused.

"A small one. She had many jewels, and by selling them one at a time, she has been able to live comfortably."

Mr. Drew nodded and glanced at his wrist watch. "I must leave now for an appointment," he said, and left the shop.

Nancy lingered. "Mr. Faber, I hope that someday Mrs. Alexandra will show me her jewel case," she said wistfully. "I did see the inside of the Easter egg. The singing nightingale is unique."

"*Singing* nightingale?" Mr. Faber echoed. "But the little bird does not sing."

"It sang for us. My friends heard the song too. However, we all thought it did not sound just right."

"That is very strange," murmured the shop owner. "When my father made the enameled egg years ago the nightingale did not sing. I shall ask Madame Alexandra about—"

At that moment there was a terrific crash against the front door. The cab of a truck burst into the shop, scattering wood and plaster. Nancy and Mr. Faber leaped to safety!

CHAPTER V

Pickpocket's Double

A LOUD groan came from the street as the truck driver stopped in the doorway. Had he hit someone?

Instantly Nancy hurried to his side. "You hurt?" Nancy asked him.

"I guess not," the man answered, "but what a mess I've made! My steering wheel went out of control."

Nancy did not wait to hear any more. She climbed over the debris to the street and glanced around to see if anyone had been injured. A woman stood looking at a ruined shopping cart of meats and groceries.

"What I do?" she wailed in broken English. "No more money for food!"

Nancy put an arm around her. "Be glad you weren't killed," she said kindly. "And I'm sure the truck driver will give you the money to buy more food and a cart. Come with me."

When the two climbed into the shop, the truck driver was asking Mr. Faber if he might use the telephone. Quickly Nancy explained the woman's plight.

"I'm sorry," the driver said. "I'll pay for the food and cart." He took out his wallet and gave her money for the total loss. The woman went off smiling.

Nancy felt she could be of no further use regarding the accident, and told Mr. Faber she would return another time. When she reached home, her thoughts reverted to Mrs. Alexandra and the singing nightingale. She decided to call on her that evening.

After reporting that she had made a little progress in searching for Francis Baum, Nancy tactfully brought up the subject of the bird.

"Oh, I think the little nightingale always has sung," Mrs. Alexandra answered. "For many years I did not realize this. Then one day I accidentally touched the spring that controls the mechanism."

"Mr. Faber thinks that his father did not intend the bird to sing."

"I fear that he is mistaken."

"Then there's no mystery connected with it?" Nancy's voice showed her disappointment.

"Not to my knowledge," Mrs. Alexandra replied. "In my life there is only one mystery. The mystery of what became of my beloved grandson. Find him for me and my gratitude will be boundless."

Mrs. Alexandra's plea stirred Nancy to greater effort in her search for the missing Francis Baum. She set off early the next morning with George and Bess to the town where the Eagle Home Service laundry was located. There she obtained the young man's new address.

"I hope he'll be there," George said excitedly.

A few minutes later the girls arrived at 35 Cornell Avenue, a guest house covered with vines. In response to their knock, a stout woman, whose hands were red and puffy from work, came to the door.

"You want to rent rooms?" she asked abruptly.

"No, we are trying to trace a young man by the name of Francis Baum," Nancy explained. "I understand he lives here."

"Yes, he rents a room upstairs," the landlady said. "But he's not here now. He had to go away for a few days on business."

Nancy was disappointed. "I believe I'll leave a message," she said. "When Mr. Baum returns tell him that I have a picture for him—one which I think he lost from his wallet. My name is Nancy Drew.

"Please ask him to call me at once in River

Heights or come for the photograph." Nancy wrote her phone number and address on a slip of paper and handed it to the woman.

"I'll tell him, but whether or not he'll do it I couldn't say," the landlady replied.

Nancy looked questioningly at her.

"Oh, he keeps so much to himself," the woman said. "It seems funny to me that he always locks his suitcase and takes the key. You can bet that man has something to conceal."

"Does Mr. Baum have many callers?"

"A man once in a while—never any girl friends," the landlady replied pointedly.

Behind Nancy's back, Bess and George giggled. It amused them that the landlady had assumed their friend was romantically interested in Francis Baum.

"Just give Mr. Baum my message, please," Nancy requested.

Blushing, she turned away, walking ahead of Bess and George, who grinned broadly.

"Now, none of your smart remarks!" Nancy said, trying to forestall any needling by the girls.

"Why, Nancy," George said in mock reproach, "we didn't know you were trying to track down a husband of royal blood!"

"Have your fun," Nancy said cheerfully.

After a leisurely lunch in an attractive restaurant on the riverbank, the girls took the ferryboat back to the opposite shore and returned to their homes. When Nancy reached hers, she found two girls seated in the living room.

"Helen Corning Archer!" Nancy greeted her old friend. "When did you and your husband get back?"

"Only yesterday," Helen answered, giving Nancy an affectionate hug and kiss, then introduced her companion as Katherine Kovna. "What an exciting trip Jim and I had in Europe!"

"I'd say you visited some of the best dress shops!" Nancy said. "That's a fantastic suit you're wearing!"

"Katherine designed and made it for me," Helen said proudly. "We met in Europe, and I talked her into coming to this country and staying with Jim and me for a while."

Nancy learned that Helen's guest hoped to open a fashion shop in town.

"Each time I go any place I'll wear a dress designed especially for me," Helen said. "Everyone will ask where I bought it, and I'll tell them of Katherine's work. The orders should roll in!"

"You Americans!" The European girl smiled. "You sweep me off the feet!" The others laughed.

"I could use a new dress," said Nancy, grinning. "Would you make one for me?"

"Katherine can measure you now," Helen said at once. "As her business manager, I accept the order. We'll give you a special discount."

Nancy went to get a tape measure from the sewing basket. Katherine made various notations on a slip of paper, and sketched a few ideas. As Nancy tried to decide which one she liked best, she casually hummed a few bars of the nightingale's song. The young designer listened attentively.

"That melody!" she murmured. "What is its name?"

"So far as I know, it has none," Nancy answered. "I'll try to sing the words, but I don't know what they mean." She sang a few syllables.

"They sound like words in my native language," Katherine announced. "But they make no meaning to me."

Nancy gazed at the girl with startled eyes. Did the nightingale's song contain a message?

"Katherine, you've given me a wonderful idea!" she exclaimed. "You may be able to help me solve a mystery!"

"I gladly do anything."

"You're a dear," Nancy said, squeezing the other's hand. "There is someone I want you to meet—Mrs. Marie Alexandra. I'll ask her if I may take you to see her tomorrow."

After the two girls had left, Nancy lost no time in telephoning Mrs. Alexandra. The woman graciously assured Nancy that she might bring her friends to tea any afternoon she chose, but asked that her real identity not be revealed.

"I should like to come tomorrow," Nancy replied and said good-by. As she stood near the phone wondering about the meeting, Mrs. Gruen called:

"Nancy, if you can descend to earth for a moment, I wish you'd go to the soda shop for some ice cream."

"Glad to," Nancy replied.

She found so many customers in the store there was a long delay before it was her turn to be waited on.

"I guess Dad will be home by the time I get back," Nancy thought as she reached the house.

She was right. His car stood in the driveway. As Nancy walked toward the kitchen door, she noticed her father in his study. She was just about to call "Hi" through the open window when she saw a frightening sight.

A man seated in a chair opposite Mr. Drew was pointing a revolver at him!

"You'll be sorry if you don't pay my price!" the man was saying to Mr. Drew.

Nancy did not wait a second. Dropping her package, she seized a rock from beneath the window and threw it at the gun. The weapon went spinning from the man's hand.

In a flash Nancy scrambled through the window, snatched up the gun, and handed it to her father.

"Why, Nancy," said Mr. Drew, "you—!"

"This man is the pickpocket who stole Francis Baum's wallet!" she told her father.

Nancy threw a rock at the gun

"No, I'm not," the man said quickly. "That gun isn't loaded, and I meant no harm."

Nancy was unconvinced, even when her father opened the weapon to show it contained no bullets.

"I guess my life wasn't in danger," Mr. Drew said, trying to relieve the situation, "but I do appreciate your trying to save me, dear."

"It's all a mistake," the caller insisted. "I came here to meet you, Miss Drew."

Nancy was bewildered. "But I did see you pointing the revolver directly at my father!"

"I was merely trying to sell the gun to him. It's a rare one."

"That's true," said Mr. Drew. "He noticed my collection of antique firearms on the wall, and thought I might like to add this one to it."

"He's wanted by the police," Nancy insisted. "Or is it possible," she said, turning to the caller, "that you're the man who looks so much like the pickpocket?"

The stranger crossed the room and she noted that he walked with a long stride and not short, quick steps.

"Yes, I am. My name is Dorrance—David Dorrance. You saved me from arrest. I asked the policeman for your name and address and came here to thank you."

"Nancy, I think you owe Mr. Dorrance an

apology," Mr. Drew said. "I'm afraid this time you've made a mistake in your sleuthing."

"I truly am sorry," she replied.

"Oh, I can't blame you for acting as you did," the caller said, accepting the revolver which Mr. Drew handed him. "I've been mistaken for that other fellow several times."

"He resembles you closely," Nancy remarked. She tried to memorize Dorrance's features to avoid any future misunderstanding.

"It's hard on me having the police and young lady detectives always after me," Dorrance resumed. "Why, your friends chased me a block, no doubt mistaking me for the pickpocket."

"Was that when you left an apartment house on Oster Street yesterday?"

"Oh, no, I haven't been near there since the day my wallet was stolen. The chase was about an hour ago."

"Why did you run?" Nancy asked.

"I didn't. It was only after I'd boarded a bus that I realized they were after me."

Nancy decided that she had been unduly suspicious of him, especially after he explained that he bought and sold antique weapons as a hobby. The revolver she had knocked from his hand had been purchased only a short time before, he said. Nancy recalled having seen a similar one at Mr. Faber's shop.

"I don't see how I made such a mistake," she said in apology. "Is there a way to avoid that happening again?"

"Why not arrange a set of signals?" Dorrance suggested, grinning.

"If I ever mistake you again for the thief, wave a handkerchief," Nancy said. "Then I'll know who you are." The young man agreed.

A moment later he left. Nancy went at once to retrieve the ice cream and placed it in the freezer, then returned to her father.

"What do you think of David Dorrance?" she asked.

"I wasn't impressed," the lawyer replied. "However, I must say he took your accusation in a rather sporting way."

Nancy perched herself on an arm of her father's chair. "I dislike him," she said. "I'll always remember that man pointing a gun at you!"

"I'm as grateful as if you'd actually saved my life, Nancy," Mr. Drew told her. "Well, here's Hannah, so dinner is ready. Let's forget this unpleasant episode," he added, tucking Nancy's arm under his own and walking to the dining room with her.

The following afternoon Nancy took Helen Archer and her house guest, Katherine, to call on Mrs. Alexandra. To Nancy's delight, the girls made a favorable impression. More than that, Katherine soon realized who the woman was, and an animated conversation between the two began at once in a foreign tongue.

"Mrs. Alexandra and I—we are from the same country," Katherine announced to the girls. "Please excuse—we have much to talk about."

The other two did not mind being excluded. They were pleased because Katherine was so happy. Nancy pointed out the various art objects in the room to Helen, who was fascinated.

Before they left, Anna, who had served tea, took the gold-encrusted Easter egg from the curio cabinet and pressed the tiny spring. The nightingale sang its strange little song.

Katherine listened attentively, but offered no comment other than polite admiration. When the three girls were on the street, Nancy eagerly asked Katherine if the bird had sung any words in her language.

"He use words of my native tongue, but they are not clear," the girl answered, frowning.

Katherine paused a moment, then she smiled. "It sound silly, maybe, but the little bird seem to say, 'clue in jewel box!' "

CHAPTER VI

True Credentials?

"YES, the nightingale say, 'clue in jewel box!' " Katherine Kovna repeated in her halting English. "But that mean nothing."

"It may mean something very important!" Nancy corrected her excitedly.

"Of course the people of my native land—they have many secrets." Katherine smiled.

The remark brought back to Nancy's mind what Mr. Faber had told her about the royal lady's escape from revolutionists with only the enameled Easter egg and a jewel box.

"There may be a connection between the two!" she said to herself. "The question is, does Mrs. Alexandra know that or not? Is the clue a political secret the woman can not reveal?"

The young detective silently considered the unexplained bits of the strange trail she was following. A pickpocket with a double had accidentally given her a clue to a lost prince. The missing man's grandmother, in turn, knowingly or unknowingly held a carefully guarded secret, judging from the trouble someone had taken to make the nightingale sing.

Nancy wondered why she had not heard from Francis Baum. If she could talk with him, some of the pieces of the puzzle might fall into place. Had Baum's landlady failed to deliver her message?

"Nancy," said Helen, breaking in on her friend's thoughts, "how would you like to model a new gown at an art and fashion show at the Woman's Club?

"Katherine has agreed to help with the fashion part of the exhibit. A special prize is to be awarded to the designer of the most original and attractive dress."

"Of course I'll do it," Nancy promised.

"It starts next Thursday. There will be three afternoon showings and one on Saturday night."

"Can you design and make a dress so soon, Katherine?" Nancy asked.

"I can try," the other replied.

"The fashion show will be a great way to have Katherine's talents recognized," went on Helen. "She ought to win first prize."

"I'm thinking of a design now—a modern one, but it have the touch of the Renaissance period,"

Katherine said dreamily. "An evening dress with a short train." She paused a moment. "Every detail I want correct."

The following afternoon Nancy went to the Archer home for the first fitting. The dress was barely started, but she could tell that it would be beautiful.

"The blue of the flowered silk exactly match your eyes," Katherine said. "I take a tuck here, and I shorten the train. Then tomorrow it is finished."

"And your reputation will be made!" Helen cried gaily. "With Nancy modeling the dress, you're certain to get many clients."

Nancy laughed. "I'll do my best."

She knew that Katherine's success meant everything to her. In the meantime, Nancy intended to devote every moment possible to finding Francis Baum.

"Why so quiet, Nancy?" Mr. Drew inquired at breakfast the next day.

His daughter had no chance to reply. From outside came a shrill scream, unmistakably the voice of Hannah Gruen.

Thoroughly alarmed, the Drews ran to the front door. A ferocious-looking German shepherd dog was jumping around and would not let the housekeeper approach the door.

"Don't come out!" the woman warned Nancy and her father. "The dog may attack you."

At that moment the animal turned of his own accord and went off. At once Hannah Gruen gained the safety of the hall.

"I was looking for the newspaper when the dog came up behind me and growled," she explained. "I'm sorry I screamed, but the animal frightened me."

"I wonder where he came from," said Nancy.

The question was answered by the arrival of a young man, who obviously was his master.

"Hope Rudy didn't frighten you," the dog's owner apologized. "He broke away from me."

The voice struck Nancy as oddly familiar. Then her heart began to beat a little faster. She recognized him as Francis Baum.

"Oh, good morning! Aren't you Mr. Baum?"

"I am," he admitted promptly. "And you are Miss Drew, who left a message for me?"

With difficulty Nancy controlled her excitement, and tried to speak in a calm, casual voice. "I have a picture which I think belongs to you."

"Of a boy in a sailor suit?"

"Yes, apparently it fell from your wallet when it was stolen."

"I'm certainly glad you found the picture. It's important," Baum replied.

"Important?" asked Nancy, trying not to show how eager she was to hear his answer.

"It may get me some relatives and a fortune someday," the man boasted.

"We'd better go inside," said Mr. Drew. "Have you had breakfast?" he inquired.

Nancy had told her father of her belief that Francis Baum was the long-missing prince.

The caller accepted quickly, his dog trailing him inside. Mrs. Gruen set an extra place at the table, all the while eying Rudy with suspicion.

Mr. Drew reopened the conversation by asking where their guest had been born. Nancy was not surprised to hear that it was in Mrs. Alexandra's native land.

"When did you come to this country, Mr. Baum?" her father inquired.

"Don't remember exactly. I was just a little kid when I was brought to America."

Nancy tried not to notice that Mr. Baum was cramming toast into his mouth and clattering the silverware noisily as he ate. Surely the nurse of a prince would have taught him better table manners!

Without any prodding, Baum added, "I wouldn't mind locating some of my real folks, but I don't know how to do it."

This was Nancy's cue to say that she might be able to help him. But she was rather dismayed to hear herself say in a tone not very friendly:

"Mr. Baum, if you have proper credentials—if you actually can prove you are the person in the photograph—I can lead you to your grandmother."

"Honestly? Where is she?" he demanded.

"I can't tell you that until you produce proof of your identity."

"I don't get it," Francis Baum said. "If you think I'm a fake—"

"Oh, I didn't mean to suggest that I doubt you," Nancy corrected hurriedly.

"Bring your credentials to us soon, Mr. Baum," said Carson Drew, his tone ending the interview. "And thank you for calling."

As soon as the young man had gone, Hannah voiced her candid opinion of him.

"If he's a lost prince, then I'm a queen! Did you see the way he gobbled his food?"

Mr. Drew frowned. "I guess he was very hungry."

Mrs. Gruen continued, "He didn't show any refinement at all!"

"He talked rather well at first," Nancy remarked. "But toward the end he almost seemed like a different person."

"You forgot to give him the lost photograph," Mr. Drew reminded her.

"I didn't forget, Dad. I decided to keep it until I'm sure of his claims."

"Then you distrust Baum?"

"Not exactly. I'll admit I don't like him. He doesn't bear the slightest resemblance to the boy in the photograph."

"Mark my words," Hannah announced flatly, "he'll never show up with any credentials."

The housekeeper's prediction proved to be wrong. Francis Baum returned, bearing a package which contained a letter written by his former nurse, and a small toy lamb with a jeweled collar. Much as she disliked to do so, Nancy felt compelled to invite the young man to stay to lunch.

"When can I see my grandmother?" Francis Baum asked Nancy as he again ate ravenously.

"Soon, I hope," she replied. "I will talk with her today, and show her the letter and the toy."

"Why can't I see her myself?" he asked sullenly.

"I have my reasons," Nancy replied. "If you expect me to help, you'll have to wait. Your credentials seem satisfactory, but only your grandmother can determine whether or not they're genuine."

"She'll recognize these things all right," he replied confidently.

Three o'clock found Nancy seated in Mrs. Alexandra's home with the letter spread out on a table between them. A lump came into her throat as she watched the woman caress the toy lamb.

"My darling grandson played with this in his nursery," the former queen said, smiling. "I gave it to him myself on his third birthday."

"And the letter? Can you identify that, too?"

Mrs. Alexandra scanned the worn sheet of paper.

"Yes, this is the handwriting of my grandson's faithful nurse, Nada. The young man *is* my lost Michael! Have him pack his belongings at once and come here to live."

CHAPTER VII

Mistaken Identity

"OH, Madame Marie!" Anna protested. "We have no room prepared for Prince Michael."

"That is true," agreed Mrs. Alexandra. "When my grandson comes, we must show him every consideration. We will have a dinner in his honor."

"Would it not be better to wait a day or two at least?" pleaded Anna.

"Very well," Mrs. Alexandra consented. "But prepare for my grandson's arrival quickly. I shall write him a letter of welcome."

Nancy ventured to suggest that it might be advisable to put away some of the most valued antiques. Anna nodded approvingly, but Mrs. Alexandra seemed displeased by the idea.

"I am sure my grandson is to be trusted," she said coldly.

"Your grandson—yes," Nancy replied. "As for this Francis Baum, you are not certain yet that he is the missing prince. His credentials seem authentic, but they might not be."

"I shall reflect upon your suggestion," Mrs. Alexandra said, her good humor restored.

Nancy was fearful that the woman would not have the treasures removed. She tried to bring up the subject of the singing nightingale and its strange message, but Mrs. Alexandra showed no willingness to discuss the matter. All her thoughts were centered upon her grandson.

"I will do what I can with Madame," Anna whispered to Nancy as the girl left the house. "But she is very determined once she makes up her mind."

The day was unusually sultry. Nancy walked slowly down the elm-shaded street. Reaching the business section, she paused to look in the window of a small shop. Suddenly the excited cries of a woman came from the next corner.

"My pocketbook!" she wailed. "That man snatched it! Stop him, someone!"

Pedestrians turned to see a young man in a brown suit running down the street, but no one acted quickly enough to stop him. Nancy saw the thief enter a department store.

"He looks like the one who stole Francis Baum's wallet—and probably Dad's!" she thought. "This is my chance to catch him!"

Confident she could have the pickpocket arrested, Nancy followed him into the department store. Although the young man mingled with the crowd, she was able to spot the thief and keep him in sight. Then, to her surprise, he turned and looked at her.

"Good afternoon, Miss Drew," he murmured. He waved a white handkerchief and smiled.

Nancy was so chagrined that she went on without a word other than a perfunctory greeting. Again she had mistaken David Dorrance for the pickpocket! She wondered if she would ever be able to make a positive identification of the thief.

The chiming of a clock reminded her that she had an appointment with Katherine to try on the blue gown. She hurried to the Archer home.

"This is the last time you'll come here for a fitting," Helen told Nancy. "Katherine's rented a shop in the arcade of the Hotel Claymore."

"It worry me," Katherine declared as she brought out the evening dress for Nancy to slip on. "The shop—Helen and Jim pay the rent."

"Now don't start all that over again," Helen said teasingly. "As soon as you're established you will be able to repay us."

The fitting proceeded. Katherine worked nimbly and seemed pleased with the Renaissance gown.

"It is perfect for you," she announced, sitting back on her heels to get a better view of Nancy. "But for your hair you need some touch—a lovely jeweled ornament."

"I don't own one," Nancy replied.

"But the dress requires it," Helen said.

"I mean a simple ornament, which fit across hair—so!" Katherine explained, holding a pair of scissors across Nancy's head to illustrate.

"Where can we get one?" Nancy asked.

"In my country it would have been so easy," declared Katherine. "Here I do not know."

"I understand what you want," Nancy said. "It's possible Mr. Faber has one."

After leaving the Archer house, she went to Mr. Faber's shop. Before explaining that she wanted to purchase a headdress, she told him that Mrs. Alexandra's grandson had been found.

"Ah, this is the happiest day of my life." The man beamed. "Ask any favor, and it is yours."

Nancy told of her need for a special hair ornament. Immediately the antique dealer searched the shelves of his little shop.

"Oh, don't put yourself to so much trouble," Nancy protested at last.

Mr. Faber pondered a moment. "You wait!" he said, moving to his desk. "I will write a note for you to take to Madame Alexandra. She has just the piece you want, and will lend it to you."

Nancy protested that she could not ask such a favor, but the shopkeeper paid no heed.

"Deliver this to Madame Alexandra," he urged. "She will gladly let you borrow the headdress. Did you not find her lost grandson?"

As Nancy turned to leave, she was startled to see a tall, bushy-haired man wearing a dark jacket standing in a shadowy corner of the shop. He was quietly examining an old print. "I wonder how long he's been there," she thought.

The following afternoon Nancy delivered Mr. Faber's message to the former queen. She read it, smiled, and then spoke rapidly to Anna in her native tongue. The servant vanished, to reappear with a sparkling ornament on a purple velvet cushion.

Nancy caught her breath. She had not expected anything so beautiful. The rubies and diamonds twinkled brilliantly.

"It is yours to keep," said Mrs. Alexandra, smiling.

Nancy protested that she could not accept such a valuable gift. It was not until she realized that her refusal was offending the woman that she agreed to wear the hair ornament in the fashion show.

"But immediately after the final showing on Saturday night I shall return it."

"Then I must find some other way to express my appreciation," Mrs. Alexandra insisted.

While Anna wrapped the jeweled hair ornament, Mrs. Alexandra eagerly talked of her grandson. What was the young man like?

Nancy was far too kind to give her true impression of him. That morning Francis Baum had phoned her to ask some questions about his grandmother. He had seemed more interested in Mrs. Alexandra's wealth than in anything else.

"Your grandson should be very happy here," she said finally.

"Everything is nearly ready now for his arrival. Anna and I will welcome him tomorrow night with a grand dinner to celebrate. I am glad that you and your father are coming."

Nancy gazed about the living room with troubled eyes. A few of the art treasures had been put away, but many remained. Fragile glass stood on small antique tables. The slightest push against them would cause disaster.

"I can't help wondering what Mr. Baum's German shepherd dog will do to this room," she remarked.

"My grandson has a dog?" Mrs. Alexandra asked.

"Yes, he has. And it isn't very well trained."

"Oh dear! I'm afraid of large dogs. What shall I do about it?"

"I'll handle the matter for you, if I may," Nancy offered. "I am certain I can induce your grandson to give up his dog."

"Oh, thank you so much," the woman said.

Relieved by Nancy's reassuring answer, the woman now spoke of Mr. Faber. She explained that his grandfather had been a distinguished personage in her country.

"Not only was he a great jeweler, but he perfected a formula for noncrackable enamel."

"But I thought no such method exists today!" Nancy exclaimed, astonished.

"Unfortunately it was lost. You must ask Mr. Faber to tell you all about it."

Mrs. Alexandra suddenly seemed weary. Nancy had intended to speak of the singing nightingale and his strange song, but decided to do so another time.

As soon as Anna appeared with the jeweled hair ornament in a paper bag, Nancy rose from her chair and said good-by.

As she left the house, the young sleuth thought, "I'm afraid Mrs. Alexandra will be disappointed when she meets her grandson."

Nancy was so busy thinking about him that she failed to observe a tall shadowy figure watching her from around the corner of the building. He nodded in satisfaction at sight of the paper bag in her hand.

Waiting until she had gone a short distance down the street, he stealthily followed Nancy.

CHAPTER VIII

Nancy Is Robbed

UNAWARE that she was being followed, Nancy walked on, deep in thought. Presently she approached a lonely section of the street, where there was an old cemetery with a high, vine-covered wall. No one was in sight, except the lone man and the unsuspecting girl toward whom he drew closer.

Suddenly the tires of a speeding automobile screeched on the roadway. Startled, Nancy turned her head to see why the driver had stopped so abruptly. As she stared at a green sedan which had pulled up at the curb, the man behind her brushed past. He jostled Nancy's arm, knocking the paper bag from her hand.

"Excuse me," he muttered. He stooped and fumbled for a moment with the bag.

"I'll get it," said Nancy quickly. Though the

man kept his head down and his face turned away, she could see he had bushy hair. Like the customer in the shop, he was tall and wore a dark jacket. Could it be the same man?

Nancy feared that he meant to steal the precious package, but he dropped it at once and hurried away. The driver of the green car alighted and picked it up for her.

"Don't you remember me?" he asked as he returned the bag. "Why, I'm an old friend!"

"You're Mr. Dorrance," Nancy said.

"That's right and I didn't even have to wave a handkerchief, did I?"

"Not this time. That pickpocket wouldn't be likely to speak to me."

"How about a lift home?" the man inquired.

Nancy politely declined the invitation. "No, thank you. I prefer to walk." She never accepted rides from persons she did not know well.

"Suit yourself." The man shrugged. He jumped into his car and quickly drove off.

"I hope my car will be fixed soon," Nancy thought and walked home without further incident. She went to the kitchen and told Hannah Gruen about borrowing the diamond-and-ruby headdress from Mrs. Alexandra.

"It's beautiful," she declared, opening the bag. "Why, it's not here!"

Dumbfounded, Nancy pulled out a dirt-covered stone.

"The ornament was stolen!" she cried, collapsing into a chair. "I've been tricked!"

"How dreadful!" said the housekeeper.

The loss made Nancy feel ill. She knew that the piece had been inside the bag when she had left Mrs. Alexandra's home. A daring thief either had substituted another bag, or else slipped the stone inside this one in place of the jewel case.

"It was either David Dorrance or that man who brushed against me!" she thought angrily.

Nancy believed that the act had been committed by the stranger who no doubt knew what she was carrying. She felt sure now that he was the man from the shop and that he had followed her. She recalled how he had shielded his face from her.

"I dread telling Mrs. Alexandra," Nancy groaned, adding, "At least I can notify the police!"

She immediately called headquarters. The lieutenant on duty assured her they would do what they could. But without a good description of the thief's face it would be more difficult to apprehend him.

"Now the next thing you must do is report the loss to Mrs. Alexandra," Hannah urged.

"I just hate to!"

"You should do it at once, Nancy."

"I know," she answered. "But it's the most disagreeable task I've ever had in my life."

Leaden feet carried her once more to the home

of Mrs. Alexandra. The woman listened in amazement to Nancy's story.

"The piece did have great value," the owner acknowledged. "A thief must have seen Anna put it into the bag. No doubt he was watching her through a window."

Nancy's spirits dropped lower, for she was afraid she might never be able to repay the great loss. At that moment Anna came into the room. Her mistress told her what had happened.

"Madame Marie," she said quickly, "the stolen ornament was not the genuine one."

"You wrapped up the imitation headdress?" the woman cried in relief. "The one Mr. Faber sold to me before he found the original family piece?"

"Yes, Madame, by mistake."

"Anna, you are the brightest of all my jewels!" the gracious lady exclaimed.

Nancy felt so grateful that she could have hugged Anna.

"I am happy the real ornament is safe," Mrs. Alexandra declared. "Since I meant you to have the genuine one, Nancy, you may take it now."

"And risk another theft? Oh no!"

"Then Anna and I will keep the headdress for you until Thursday, if you prefer."

Nancy rose to leave. "And when I come for it, I may bring a bodyguard!" Her eyes twinkled as she added, "As for your dinner party tomorrow evening, my father and I will bring only your grandson!"

Dinner was ready by the time Nancy reached home. Mrs. Gruen had prepared an excellent meal, but for some reason Carson Drew ate little.

"What's wrong, Dad?" Nancy inquired, glancing up. "Aren't you feeling well?"

"Oh, I'm all right."

"Then you're worried. Is it about that wallet you lost?"

"Well, I had hoped it would be returned," the lawyer admitted. "At least the papers in it."

"You ran an ad in the newspaper, didn't you?"

"Yes, I offered a reward and no questions asked. Nothing came of it."

"I've had no luck in tracing the pickpocket either," Nancy said, sighing.

At that moment the discussion was interrupted by the ringing of the doorbell. Nancy went to answer it. At the door stood a good-looking young man, broad-shouldered and deeply tanned.

"Ned!" Nancy cried jubilantly. "It's great to see you!"

"And you." He laughed, seizing her hand. "I just happened to be doing an errand near here and thought I'd drop over."

Ned Nickerson and Nancy were friends of long standing. They enjoyed the same things and frequently went together to parties. Though she had many other admirers, Nancy admitted to herself that Ned was her favorite.

"Are you free for a date tonight?" he asked.

"I have one," Nancy said with genuine regret. "Why didn't you warn me you were coming?"

"How about tomorrow night?"

"Mrs. Alexandra, a new acquaintance, has invited Dad and me to a special dinner party. We are to take her grandson, Francis Baum, to see her for the first time. It's thrilling, Ned! He's supposed to be a missing prince—"

"Wish he'd stay missing," Ned muttered. "Well, how about tomorrow afternoon?"

"Fine, if you'll get me home in time to dress for the dinner party."

"All right, we'll take in the carnival," Ned said. "Everything from fortune-telling to the roller coaster."

The following afternoon the two arrived at the carnival grounds. They mingled with the crowd, enjoying the various amusements.

Finally Ned bought tickets for the roller coaster. As the car dashed madly down each incline, Nancy held her breath and clung to Ned. He enjoyed this so much that he suggested a second ride.

"No, let's try something else," Nancy pleaded. "How about the Ferris wheel?"

"Too tame."

"After that wild ride I crave something mild."

"Then up we go," Ned gave in reluctantly.

He bought tickets, and they sat down in one of the cars. Soon the giant wheel began to turn. It moved very slowly. The motor which rotated it made a loud, racking noise.

"Terrible!" Ned complained. "Sounds as if it's going to fall apart!"

"It's pokey, too," Nancy admitted. "Oh, well, the torture won't last long."

Just then the Ferris wheel came to a grinding halt. The car in which Nancy and Ned were seated remained stationary at the very top. Minutes elapsed, but still the wheel did not start.

"What's the matter with this thing?" Ned demanded, peering over the side.

Below, he could see two men working over the machinery. Persons in the lower cars close to the ground were being helped out.

"We're stuck up here!" Ned exclaimed.

CHAPTER IX

Ferocious Dog

"THEY'LL fix it soon," Nancy said. "In the meantime, let's enjoy the view."

"The sun's hot and I'm thirsty."

"We might ask one of the men to pass us up some cool drinks," Nancy suggested.

"Now that's a cool idea," Ned said, grinning.

He called to the men below, asking them to send up both food and drink by means of long poles, which could be handed from car to car. Other trapped passengers took up the cry.

At first the request was looked upon as a joke, but as time wore on and the wheel did not move, Ned asked a second time. Others added their pleas, and finally they were answered.

After another hour had elapsed, Ned teased Nancy, "Still enjoying the view?"

"It's getting monotonous," she said, shifting

into a more comfortable position. She glanced at her watch worriedly. "If I don't get home soon, I'll be late for Mrs. Alexandra's dinner."

Ned replied soberly, "Wish I could do something."

"I asked Francis Baum to come to our house at six-thirty," Nancy put in restlessly. "Katherine Kovna has been invited, too," she added, and told Ned about the designer.

"I guess the workmen expect to get the machinery fixed any minute now," Ned said a little later to encourage her. "Cheer up!"

Nancy settled back into her seat again, forcing herself to remain calm. Her gaze roved to the curious crowd which had gathered some distance away to stare at the motionless Ferris wheel. As she idly watched, a wiry built man, who walked with short, quick steps, edged close to another man. Deftly he removed a wallet from the hip pocket of the unsuspecting victim and turned to slip away in the crowd.

"Ned!" Nancy exclaimed, clutching his hand. "I just saw a pickpocket take a man's wallet! We must do something!"

"What can we do?"

Together they shouted, trying to attract the attention of someone on the ground. But other trapped passengers were making so much noise that no one paid any attention.

"It's no use now," Nancy said. "The pickpocket's gone, and we'll probably be here forever! Oh—"

Suddenly the Ferris wheel began to move. The cars jerked violently.

"Here we go!" Ned exclaimed jubilantly.

The next instant the cars raced downward at a breath-taking speed. The machinery was completely out of control!

The Ferris wheel made a complete revolution, stopping with a terrific jerk. Once more the car in which Ned and Nancy were imprisoned stopped at the top.

"That was horrible!" Nancy exclaimed.

In the car beneath them two little girls began to whimper with fear. The younger child stood up and started to unfasten the safety bar.

"I won't stay on this thing another minute!" she screamed hysterically.

Nancy, thoroughly alarmed, leaned far over. She spoke to the frightened children soothingly.

"Just look!" Nancy said cheerfully. "A photographer has come to take your picture."

The prospect of having their pictures taken on the Ferris wheel took the children's minds off their predicament. They sat down again and even smiled as the shutter clicked.

A moment later the Ferris wheel started to revolve. Everyone sat tense, fearful of another wild ride. But this time the cars moved slowly and one by one came to a stop. The passengers alighted.

"At last!" breathed Nancy as she and Ned were released. "If we hurry, I can still reach home in time to change for dinner."

"Just a minute!" interposed the photographer.

Before Nancy could duck her head, he had snapped the picture.

"The nerve of that guy!" Ned exclaimed.

Nancy laughed to cover her irritation. "I really must get home!"

The couple soon reached the Drew house.

"I wish you had been invited to the dinner, Ned," Nancy said regretfully.

"All I ask is that you don't pay too much attention to that prince." He chuckled. "I'll pick you up for Helen's picnic. 'Bye."

As he drove away, a taxi drew up nearby. Katherine Kovna, dressed in a white evening gown with matching coat and beaded bag, alighted at the curb. She was alone because Helen and Jim Archer, although invited, had been unable to accept.

"Am I early?" Katherine inquired.

"You're exactly on time," Nancy replied. "I'm the offender. But it won't take me long to change."

After explaining briefly what had occurred, she led Katherine into the house. Mr. Drew was just coming down the stairway, very handsome in his navy-blue dinner jacket and bow tie.

"Nancy, what delayed you?" he asked.

Again Nancy offered her excuses. Mrs. Gruen, entering the room, urged her to hurry.

"Isn't Francis Baum here?" Nancy asked as she took the stairs two steps at a time.

"Not yet," her father answered.

Nancy was ready in record time. As she surveyed herself in a long mirror, she decided that the pale tangerine gown was attractive and appropriate.

"Baum still hasn't arrived," Mr. Drew said when Nancy appeared. "Are you sure he understood he was to come to our house?"

"Oh, yes, Dad. I called him this morning."

Mrs. Gruen, who stood at the front door, said, "Someone's coming down the street. He's dressed in sports shirt and slacks, though."

"Then it couldn't be Mr. Baum," Nancy replied. "He'd be wearing dinner clothes."

"All the same, it looks like him. He has a suitcase and a German shepherd dog!"

"A dog!" Nancy's face darkened. "I can't believe he brought that animal! I told him that his grandmother is afraid of large dogs."

Darting to the window, she saw that the young man approaching was indeed Francis Baum.

"Guess I'm a little late," he remarked, stepping into the hall.

"Why did you bring the dog?" Nancy asked.

"Can't I take him along?"

"I don't think your grandmother would want Rudy at her dinner party."

"Well, then I'll have to leave him here."

"Here?" Hannah Gruen asked sharply.

"Just overnight. He's harmless."

"I won't be here to look after him," the housekeeper said coldly. "I'm going to a movie."

"Oh, he can stay outside," Francis Baum said carelessly. "I'll tie him by the garage."

He seemed unaware that he had caused the slightest inconvenience.

"I suppose you're eager to see your grandmother," Mr. Drew remarked.

"Oh, sure," he replied, but his tone lacked warmth. "What's she like?"

"Decidedly formal," Nancy warned him.

"Maybe she won't let me eat with you in these clothes." He grinned. "But she'll soon like me."

Nancy avoided looking at her father and Katherine. They all felt sick at heart, knowing that Mrs. Alexandra could not fail to be disappointed upon meeting her grandson.

Mr. Drew parked in front of the house, which glowed with lights, and followed the others to the door. It was opened by Anna.

Upon entering, Mr. Drew's gaze wandered to an unusual card tray on the hall table. Constructed of copper, it was decorated with colored bits of enamel in a flower-and-leaf design.

"That's a sample of wonderful old enamel work," he said to Nancy.

"You'll see many other treasures, unless they have been put away," she said.

In the living room Mrs. Alexandra, gowned in rich maroon velvet trimmed with real lace, greeted her guests. Her eyes were moist as she kissed Francis Baum on either cheek. If his appearance startled her, she did not show it.

"Michael," she said tenderly, leading him to a sofa, "I have prayed we would be reunited."

"I'm glad to know you," he replied. "But I thought my name was Francis. Guess Mom was afraid to call me Michael."

Nancy thought she detected a slight start on the part of her hostess. It seemed strange that his nurse would have had a royal child call her "Mom."

"Michael Alexandra is your true name," the former queen explained. "Do you recall anything of life at the palace?"

Francis squirmed uncomfortably. "I remember seeing some parades. That's all."

An awkward pause followed. It was broken by Anna announcing dinner. As the double doors of the dining room were opened, Nancy drew in her breath at the beautiful table setting. Orchids formed the centerpiece, the cloth was made of rare lace, and at each place was a name card.

Francis Baum found his chair at once and sat

down without waiting for the others. To cover his mistake, Mrs. Alexandra quickly seated herself. It was evident to all that she meant to spare her grandson embarrassment.

The first course was a compote of rare fruits served in fragile hand-blown glass cups. The service plates were of rich dark blue and gold, with hand-painted bouquets. The handles of the knives and forks were inlaid with mother-of-pearl.

Nancy and Katherine were so impressed by all the splendor that they felt as if they were dining in fairyland. A glance at Francis Baum, however, brought them to earth quickly. The young man made one mistake after another, both in his table manners and in his attempts at conversation.

"He certainly has forgotten everything he ever was taught," thought Nancy.

Dessert was served on dainty plates of salmon pink and gold. Their decorations of enamel were so unusual that Mr. Drew commented on the fine work.

"It is indeed remarkable," Mrs. Alexandra admitted, pleased by his interest. "At one time, only the ladies of the court had dessert served on these plates." She smiled. "But now I am sharing this secret with you gentlemen."

She turned to Francis Baum. "Michael dear, do tell us something of your life here in America," she urged gently.

"Nothing to tell," he mumbled, avoiding her

gaze. "I didn't have a chance to get much education—too busy working."

"You shall have an opportunity to learn now, Michael. You'll have a tutor."

"I'll need to find out how to handle myself in society," the young man admitted. "You can teach me the ropes yourself, though. Right?"

Mrs. Alexandra looked slightly distressed at her grandson's crude remarks. The next instant she smiled. Arising, she indicated that the long dinner had ended.

The guests returned to the living room, from which many art treasures had been removed. The Easter egg, too, had disappeared. Nancy was disappointed that her father would not have an opportunity to hear the nightingale's song.

Realizing that Mrs. Alexandra no doubt wished to be alone with her grandson, the guests soon offered excuses for leaving. Francis Baum followed Nancy into the hall and whispered:

"How about you and me having a date soon?"

"Thank you, I'll be very busy—for some time," Nancy said.

"Oh, do it as a favor to my grandmother."

Nancy was glad that Mrs. Alexandra's appearance in the hall at that moment made it unnecessary for her to reply. The Drews and Katherine departed, leaving Baum in his new home.

"It's difficult to believe that he's related to Madame Alexandra," Nancy said to Mr. Drew after taking Katherine to the Archer residence. "If Mrs. Alexandra hadn't been so firmly convinced that his credentials were authentic, I'd have thought he was an impostor."

"Training may make young Baum into a new person," Mr. Drew declared. "Let's hope so."

When they reached home, Mr. Drew went directly to the garage. He and Nancy alighted. The windows in the house were dark, evidence that Mrs. Gruen had not returned.

As the Drews neared the side door, they were startled to hear an angry growl. Baum's dog had broken away from the rope and was crouched on the top step, ready to leap on Nancy and her father.

"Let's try the front door," she suggested.

The annoying animal followed them. He became increasingly unfriendly, and would not let them come within several yards of the entrance.

"What'll we do, Dad?"

"It's too late to telephone the dog warden."

"We can't stay outdoors!" said Nancy.

Mr. Drew nodded grimly.

"I know what we'll do," he said with satisfaction. "Just follow me, Nancy."

CHAPTER X

Amazing Revelation

MR. DREW led the way to the home of their neighbor Mr. Gleason. Grimly he told Nancy that he would call Francis Baum and ask him to come for his dog at once.

"That's a good idea," she agreed.

The owner of the animal was not cooperative. But when Mr. Drew remained firm, Baum reluctantly agreed to take him away.

"Who does that fellow think he is, anyway?" the lawyer demanded.

"Merely a prince." Nancy giggled. "Since he has the title, he feels he should act the part."

"Putting other people to a lot of trouble is anything but princely!" her father declared. "Why don't you wait here at the Gleasons, Nancy?" he suggested. "I'll walk back and watch for Baum."

"I wouldn't desert you." She snuggled close to him. "His Royal Highness will arrive soon."

Minutes elapsed and Mr. Drew became more impatient. Again he tried to get into the house, but the dog became even more ferocious. After nearly an hour had gone by, he announced he would telephone the young man again. At that instant a taxi came down the street and stopped.

"There he is now!" the lawyer muttered.

"I was just ready to go to bed when you called," Baum complained as he reached the Drews. "Couldn't you handle Rudy without bothering me?"

"I could have turned him over to the police," the lawyer retorted testily.

Francis Baum called the dog, who responded readily to his master. He loaded the animal into the taxi and left without a word of apology.

"Dad, I'm afraid you weren't very polite to the prince," Nancy said teasingly.

"I've had enough of that young man," Mr. Drew replied. "In fact, if I never meet him again, I will be pleased."

Mr. Drew yawned upon entering the house. "Think I'll turn in immediately. I've had a big day."

"Me too," Nancy added wearily. "Those hours on the Ferris wheel wore me out."

Going at once to her room, Nancy undressed and tumbled into bed. She did not even hear Mrs. Gruen, who arrived home only a few minutes later. Nancy slept until nine o'clock the next morning, when the housekeeper entered the bedroom.

"Good morning, Nancy. I didn't expect to see your picture in today's paper."

"What!" Nancy asked, sitting bolt upright.

"Just look at the front page." Hannah handed her the newspaper.

The *River Heights Gazette* carried a three-column picture of Nancy and Ned, their heads lowered, as they obviously fled from photographers. A headline proclaimed:

NANCY DREW SAVES CHILD FROM FALL

"How horrible!" Nancy exclaimed. "With the fashion show starting Thursday, people will think I'm looking for publicity."

"Not those who know you," Mrs. Gruen said kindly.

With the show almost at hand, Nancy had no time to think more about the incident. Immediately after breakfast she attended a rehearsal at the Woman's Club with Katherine, Helen, Bess, and George. Beautiful paintings hung on the walls and many gorgeous ensembles were on display.

"But there's not an entry to compare with the Kovna–Drew combination," Helen Archer assured the girls confidently.

"I hope you're right," Nancy replied. "The competition will be keen."

Although Katherine had declared the gown finished, she kept adding touches.

"I think I make loops of the dress material to swing gracefully from the back of your head," she explained.

"I'll feel like a young queen!" Nancy said, laughing.

To complete the elaborate headdress, Katherine needed the ornament that Mrs. Alexandra had promised to lend. Bess and George offered to accompany Nancy to get it.

"We'll make sure that no thief outwits you this time!" George promised.

On the way to Mrs. Alexandra's home, the girls stopped at Mr. Faber's shop to say hello. He said that on the previous day he had been told by the police how the imitation ruby-and-diamond headpiece had been snatched from Nancy and decided to do some investigating. The girls were startled when he placed the ornament on the show counter.

"Why, Mr. Faber, where did you get this?" Nancy asked in astonishment.

"From a pawnbroker just a little while ago."

"Then the man who snatched it from me must have pawned it!"

"Yes. The police are trying to track him down."

Smiling, Mr. Faber placed the hair ornament in a padded case and gave it to Nancy.

With the imitation ornament once more in her possession, Nancy remarked that it would not be necessary for her to borrow the original.

"You make a mistake if you do not wear the genuine piece," Mr. Faber advised. "This one does not sparkle as much as the original."

The girls left the shop and continued to Mrs. Alexandra's house. Nancy gave her the headdress and told how it had been recovered.

"I am glad for you," the former queen said with a smile. "Now you will not be worried about it."

The girls had hoped to talk with her alone, so they were disappointed to find Francis Baum there. He explained that he now had much leisure time.

"It's not fitting for a prince to work," he declared loftily.

"Michael will need time for his studies," Mrs. Alexandra said. "I hope to engage a tutor for him within a few days."

"No hurry about it," the young man interposed. "I want to have a good time for a while."

Bess and George noticed that many art treasures had been removed from the living room. Nancy had forgotten to tell them that Anna had put away the objects until the two women became better acquainted with the newcomer.

"Where is the Easter egg?" Bess asked.

Francis Baum became immediately alert. "Easter egg?" he demanded. "What's that?"

"Merely one of the things I brought with me when I came to this country."

"Let's see what it's like."

Mrs. Alexandra ordered Anna to bring the little treasure. She obeyed reluctantly.

Francis Baum's eyes brightened at the sight of the Easter egg with the gold-encrusted lid. He raised the lid. Beholding the nightingale, he astonished everyone by asking if it could sing.

"Then you too know the secret!" Mrs. Alexandra exclaimed.

She took the beautiful ornament from him. At the touch of her finger the nightingale sang its song. The young man gave no hint that he understood the words.

Mrs. Alexandra told the story of her escape from her country, much the same as Nancy had heard it from Mr. Faber.

"Michael dear, what did your nurse tell you about the nightingale?" she asked.

"Just about what you've told me. Why do you keep asking me?"

As if to escape further questioning, the young man arose and hurriedly left the room.

Nancy quickly told Mrs. Alexandra that Katherine thought the nightingale might be saying in her native tongue, "clue in jewel box."

The former queen touched the secret spring several times. Finally she admitted that the little bird might be trying to convey such a message.

"Do you know what it means?" Nancy asked.

Before Mrs. Alexandra could reply, they were startled by a loud crash. From the kitchen Anna's voice was raised in fright and anger.

"Oh, Michael!" they heard her wail. "What have you done now?"

Mrs. Alexandra and the three girls, alarmed by Anna's cries, hastened to the kitchen. On the floor lay a porcelain bowl which had broken into a dozen pieces.

"Madame Marie, it was not my fault!" Anna said, her eyes fastened on Michael.

"No, blame me!" he retorted sharply. "Sure I did it. So the old bowl cracked."

"Old? Cracked?" Anna's voice rose in anger. "That lovely porcelain cannot be replaced. The king gave it to Madame. She—"

"There, Anna, please say no more," Mrs. Alexandra interrupted. "It was an accident. After all, my grandson is far more precious to me than the most valuable piece of porcelain."

"That's the way to talk, Grandmother!" Michael nodded. "I'll get you another bowl."

It was easy to see that Mrs. Alexandra felt deeply distressed. Nevertheless, she passed the matter off with regal composure. Nancy decided it was not the right time to bring up the subject

"I'm afraid to borrow it," Nancy said

again of the nightingale's mysterious reference to a jewel box.

"We must leave now," she said considerately. "May I take the hair ornament that Mr. Faber recovered?"

To her dismay, Mrs. Alexandra asked Anna to bring in the genuine headdress and place it on Nancy's head.

"It suits you perfectly. You must wear it in the fashion show," she insisted.

Nancy did not want to offend the woman a second time, yet she was fearful that something would happen to the tiara-like piece.

"I'm really afraid to borrow it," she declared dubiously.

"Do take it to please me," Mrs. Alexandra urged. "I assume all responsibility. Anna will wrap it for you."

Nancy thanked the woman, and left the house with Bess and George. They carried the precious package at once to Katherine.

"Ah, it will set off the Renaissance costume!" the designer approved in delight. "I ask Jim to put the ornament in his safe!"

"Fine. See you at the picnic this afternoon."

"It is sweet of Helen to give it for me," Katherine said with a smile.

After picking up her car at the service station, she dropped Bess and George at their homes, then stopped at police headquarters to find out if there was any news of the pickpocket. Chief McGinnis said that a suspect had just been brought in for questioning.

"May I see him?" Nancy requested.

"Certainly," the officer replied.

Well acquainted with both Nancy and her father, he frequently received useful clues and tips from them. In fact, Nancy had solved so many cases that the chief jokingly declared Nancy to be an unofficial member of his staff!

The man who had been captured was placed in a line-up with other suspects. Nancy studied each person as he stood on a platform under a powerful light. The wiry built pickpocket she had hoped to identify was not in the group.

"Sorry," she said regretfully. "I've never seen any of these people before."

As Nancy was about to leave the building, an irate man burst in.

"You policemen!" he fairly shouted. "I've been paying taxes here for twelve years, and what do I get in return? Nothing! When I need a policeman, I can't find one! And when I finally get one, he arrests the wrong man!"

CHAPTER XI

The Island Trick

"If you have a complaint to make, the lieutenant will take it—over at that desk," a sergeant told the complaining man.

He calmed down a bit and directed his remarks to the chief. In a bitter voice he revealed that his wallet had been snatched while he was standing in front of a store.

He had shouted for a policeman. The officer had arrested a man, who immediately established his innocence. Shortly afterward the wallet, empty, had been found in an alley.

"You can bet the thief had an accomplice," the angry victim declared. "When the policeman came on the run, I heard someone in the crowd whistle as if in warning."

"You did not see the person who whistled?"

"No, I didn't."

The lieutenant promised he would do what he

could, and made a routine report. After the indignant man had left headquarters, the officer gazed rather apologetically at Nancy.

"What can we do?" he asked with a shrug. "Money can't be traced, unless the bills were marked or the serial numbers recorded."

Chief McGinnis said, "Nancy, I believe you'll have to turn your talents to this case." There was a twinkle in the eyes of the good-natured officer.

"Too busy today," she joked in return.

Homeward bound, Nancy began to wonder whether this latest theft had been committed by the same man who had stolen her father's wallet, and who was also responsible for the purse snatchings in River Heights.

"Somehow I must recover the money for the Boys Club, and the valuable papers Dad lost!" she thought resolutely. "This afternoon, I'll be at Helen's picnic for Katherine. Maybe tomorrow a new clue will come my way!"

The young people were to go by motorboat far up the river to Star Island. The outing promised to be an especially enjoyable one.

Ned Nickerson came for Nancy in his car. Upon reaching the dock, the couple found that the other picnickers had arrived ahead of them. Ned's college friend Bob Dutton escorted Katherine. George Fayne and an athletic young man, Burt Eddleton, had come together, and Bess had brought her favorite date, Dave Evans.

"Everyone is here," Helen declared, counting all of her guests, who numbered twelve.

Two motorboats, to be operated by Jim Archer and Ned, had been rented for the outing. The passengers were divided between the crafts, and Jim started off. The ropes of Ned's craft were about to be cast off when a shout came from shore.

"Hey, wait a minute!" Francis Baum ran to the dock, followed by his dog. Thinking that he might have a message for her from his grandmother, Nancy asked Ned to wait. In a low voice she told him that the newcomer was Mrs. Alexandra's grandson.

"What's up? A boat trip?" the prince demanded as he reached the group.

"You guessed it," Ned answered shortly.

"How about taking me along?"

"The boats are filled now. Otherwise—" Dave started to say.

"Oh, you can make room for me," Michael insisted, jumping aboard and squeezing in between Nancy and Bess.

The dog also leaped into the craft. Before he could be made to lie down, he had put his dirty paws on Bess's beige slacks, soiling them badly.

"Oh!" she cried out.

"Hey, pitch that beast out on the dock!" Ned ordered. "We're not going to take him."

Nancy was concerned that Mrs. Alexandra might be hurt if the prince told her about the boys' attitude. She nudged Ned, and he became silent. She now presented Michael to the group, being careful not to reveal the identity of Mrs. Alexandra.

"Why don't you tell your friends I'm really Prince Michael?" he urged. "It's not everybody who has a queen for a grandmother."

Those in the group who did not know the story looked at him in amusement. They thought he was joking, and Nancy made no comment.

"How did you know about our picnic?" she asked quietly.

"I didn't," he said with a grin. "I just happened to be walking my dog down here. Lucky, wasn't it?" No one replied.

As they edged away from the dock, a sleek speedboat cruised past. Beside its driver, who was a sad-faced young man, sat a little boy. Michael ducked low.

"Is he afraid of being seen by that other man?" Nancy asked herself.

As the trip proceeded, Bess, Ned, and their friends paid little attention to Michael. They had started singing. Nancy, crowded by the dog, presently climbed over the seat, and perched herself on the afterdeck of the boat.

"Lots of room back here!" she shouted.

The others continued to sing and did not join her. She became interested in watching the speedboat, which was about to pass them again.

It was not until the channel buoy had been rounded that Bess glanced over her shoulder. Then she screamed.

"Stop the boat, Ned! Quickly! Nancy's gone! She must have fallen overboard!"

Ned swung the motorboat in a wide arc, while the worried young people looked across the water. They saw a figure swimming some distance away.

"It's Nancy!" cried Bess, pointing. "She's holding up a little boy!"

Another boat also was speeding toward the scene. Ned, however, was the first to reach Nancy. Many hands pulled her and the little boy aboard. Immediately he began to cry.

"You're all right," Nancy said, putting her arms around him and hugging him close to her.

Between sobs the boy said, "Mr. Ellington's going to scold me for falling off his boat."

Both Nancy and Ned hastened to console the boy. "Oh no! He knows it was just an accident that could happen to anybody."

"Look, here is your boat now," Nancy said as it drew alongside.

"That's Mr. Ellington," the boy said, pointing to the handsome man at the wheel.

The man looked frightened as he realized by what a narrow margin a tragedy had been averted.

"You had him before I knew he was overboard," he said shakily. "If anything had happened to Buddy Farrell, I couldn't have faced his parents," he declared. "He's the son of the superintendent of the apartment house where I live."

Buddy was handed over to Mr. Ellington. As the two boats separated, Nancy remarked that the sad-faced young man seemed very nice.

"Too stiff to suit me," cut in Michael.

"Mr. Ellington is a talented commercial artist," said Katherine. "I see some of his drawings at an exhibit. He sell them, I think, to magazines. Helen say he will be at the fashion show, and I must make impression on him!"

"What is his first name?" Nancy asked.

"I do not know. He sign all his drawings R. H. Ellington."

Star Island soon came into view, and the boat was tied to a dock near a sandy beach. Helen and Jim's group already had arrived. All the young men except Michael offered to carry the picnic hampers to a spot among the trees.

Nancy introduced Michael to the others, then said, "Let's go for a swim!"

"The prince will have a chance to show us his skill," Ned added.

Michael smiled in a superior way. "Sorry, I didn't bring swim trunks."

"I'll let you have mine," Jim offered. "We're about the same size."

"No, thank you," the young man declined. "I never wear anybody else's clothing."

The others felt certain that he was giving these lame excuses because he was a poor swimmer. While they dived and raced in a sheltered cove, he amused himself by throwing sticks into the water for his dog to retrieve.

"Can't you play that little game somewhere else?" Ned demanded crossly.

"So sorry," Michael replied, but he kept on throwing sticks in the swimming area.

"I've had my fill of that guy!" Ned muttered.

"So have I," added Bob Dutton.

Out of earshot of Nancy they formed a plan to be put into effect if Michael should annoy them any more. The young people decided to dress. Nancy's clothing had dried.

The girls were ready first and began to set out the lunch. Michael took several sandwiches for his dog without asking permission.

"I wish those boys would hurry," Helen said after fifteen minutes had gone by.

Presently the youths turned up, broad grins on their faces. Nancy suspected they were up to some trick.

As the food was passed, it became evident that the prince had not learned anything about good manners from his association with his grandmother. He was as greedy as ever.

"Michael," said Ned, addressing him abruptly, "will you do us a favor?"

"What is it?" Michael asked suspiciously.

"Katherine left her coat in the motorboat. Dash down and get it for her," Ned replied, giving the girl a wink.

The young man considered a moment, and then smiled at Katherine. "I'll do it for *you*. But when I get back, I'll expect a reward."

"You'll get it," Ned promised.

As Michael started toward the beach with his dog, Nancy glanced questioningly at Ned. Instantly the boys arose and hurriedly stuffed the remaining food into the hampers.

"We pulled the motorboats to another dock," he explained. "Here's where we leave Prince Charming! Come on!" Ned urged. "A ferryboat touches Star Island every two hours. His highness can get home on that."

Nancy felt that they should not desert the young man, but was overruled. Keeping out of sight, the young people slipped down to the dock and boarded the two boats. The roar of the motors brought Michael sprinting madly along the beach.

"Hey, wait for me!" he shouted.

"Can't hear you," Bob called through cupped hands. "Louder!"

Michael shouted again and again. Finally, as the boats sped away, he slumped down on the beach.

"It was a mean trick—" Nancy began, but Ned interrupted her.

"He deserved it. Don't waste any of your sympathy on him. Save it for Mrs. Alexandra."

When the young people reached River Heights, they all went to a movie.

The next morning Nancy dropped in to see Mr. Faber about her father's birthday gift. The antique dealer said, "I think I have found just the right gentleman's box for Mr. Drew."

He showed her a handsome brown leather chest trimmed with silver.

"It's beautiful!" she said and lifted the lid. "And in wonderful condition," she added, gazing at the velvet-lined trays for jewelry.

"I hope your father likes it," he said anxiously. "Madame Alexandra asked me to make a special effort to please him."

"How nice of her!" Nancy exclaimed. "Have you seen her recently?"

"No, but Michael was here early this morning."

"Michael?"

"Yes, he brought me a ring to sell for Madame Alexandra." Mr. Faber's face became troubled. "I gave her the best price I could, but it worries me that she must sell her treasures."

"Maybe Prince Michael is an expensive grandson to have," Nancy remarked.

"Ah, yes!" Mr. Faber said with concern. "It is a pity Madame can deny him nothing."

When Nancy reached home, Mrs. Gruen gave her an urgent message from Anna.

"She called twice," the housekeeper said. "Mrs. Alexandra is very troubled. Anna wants you to come at once."

"Of course I'll go," Nancy agreed. "I wonder if Michael had anything to do with her condition."

A few minutes later she arrived at the Downey Street home and asked Anna if he had been the cause of Mrs. Alexandra's agitation.

"I don't see how Michael can be responsible," the maid replied. "He has been away most of the morning."

"He was at Mr. Faber's," Nancy said. "I thought maybe his selling the ring for Mrs. Alexandra might have upset her."

"Michael sold a ring for Madame Marie?" Anna's eyes opened wide at this bit of news.

"Didn't you know about it?" Nancy asked.

"I certainly did not!" Anna returned with displeasure. "If I had known— But now it is too late. Madame Marie has spent money most lavishly the past couple of days."

"Is Michael here now?" Nancy asked.

"He came in about ten minutes ago," the woman replied. "He tied up that dog of his, and went off somewhere. He was in a dreadful mood."

"Did he tell you what had disturbed him?"

"Only that some acquaintances of his had left him stranded on an island yesterday," Anna continued. "A fisherman took him off in a small boat.

He had to row part of the way to shore, and blistered his hands.

"I am glad it happened," Anna declared, her black eyes flashing. "Michael will require many lessons to make a gentleman of him."

"May I see Mrs. Alexandra now?" Nancy asked.

As the two started upstairs, the dog began to bark. The disturbance was so loud that Nancy and Anna hastened to a window to see what was wrong. To their dismay, the huge animal had broken the rope and was attacking the mailman.

"Oh! Oh!" moaned Anna, covering her eyes.

Nancy ran out the front door, determined to help the man. Her eye fell on the garden hose ready for use on the lawn. Unable to reach the faucet to turn on the water, she seized the hose and tried to lash at the dog.

"Run!" she shouted.

The mailman scrambled into the vestibule, his uniform ripped from the knees down.

Nancy whirled and faced the animal defiantly. With a snarl he made a leap for her face.

CHAPTER XII

A Puzzling Secret

NANCY might have been bitten by the vicious dog if the letter carrier had not acted quickly. As she dodged the animal, the man leaped from the vestibule, seized the hose from her hand and beat off the dog.

Nancy ran toward the cellar door and yanked it open. When the animal followed her, she got behind the door. As he shot down the cellar stairs Nancy slammed the door shut. He was trapped!

In the meantime, the letter carrier examined his torn trouser legs. "Are you the owner?" he asked Nancy.

"He belongs to Mrs. Alexandra's grandson."

"The dog must be turned over to the authorities."

"I agree with you," Nancy said. "If he's allowed to stay here, someone may be bitten. I'll call the dog warden at once."

Anna, who had witnessed the scene from indoors, offered no objection to the decision.

"The dog has greatly upset Madame Marie. It should go," Anna said quietly.

Nancy telephoned the city pound, and presently a man arrived to take away the dangerous animal. Rudy resisted capture, but eventually was subdued.

"It is a great relief," Anna sighed as she prepared a tray of food for her mistress.

A bell in the kitchen jingled. Anna explained, "It is Madame Marie. Come and see her."

Nancy followed Anna upstairs to a large room. The walls were draped with silk hangings, the floor covered with a beautiful Oriental rug. A canopy of blue velvet with gold fringe hung above a large four-poster bed that had graceful figures of swans carved on the headboard.

"This is a queen's room indeed," thought Nancy as she and the woman exchanged greetings.

Mrs. Alexandra, her face pale, tossed restlessly on a lace-covered pillow.

"Anna, why were you so long in coming?"

"I came as quickly as I could, Madame. There was a slight disturbance—"

"The dog?"

"Yes, but he will annoy you no more."

"I am so glad. His constant barking makes my head ache." She went on, "Anna, bring my clothing. I cannot remain any longer in bed."

"But, Madame, you must rest. I will bring your luncheon tray."

"I have no appetite."

"I'll sit beside you while you eat," Nancy offered, "and you can tell me of life at court."

She knew that the woman frequently forgot her present troubles while talking of happy past events.

"I will taste the food," Mrs. Alexandra murmured politely.

Nancy and Anna raised the woman up in bed, bracing her with cushions. The maid then brought water in a silver basin. After washing her mistress's hands, she dried them on a towel of fine linen. The woman's initials and a royal crown were embroidered on it.

At first Mrs. Alexandra ate sparingly. But as Nancy encouraged her to talk about life at the palace before the start of the Revolution, she seemed to forget her unhappiness. Soon she had finished the entire meal.

"Madame Marie, would you not enjoy showing Miss Nancy a few of your things?" Anna said, delighted that her mistress's spirits were lifting. "The orchid silk sachet bags we use to scent your clothing, for instance?"

"I should love to see them—everything!" Nancy said.

At a nod from Mrs. Alexandra, Anna brought one of the perfumed little bags and laid it in

Nancy's hand. It was decorated with a hand-embroidered monogram.

"And here is one of Madame Marie's handkerchiefs," Anna said. She was holding a dainty square of white batiste, embroidered in brown, with a lace border. "The skillful mendings were made by Madame herself," the maid explained.

"Even queens in my country are taught to be thrifty." Mrs. Alexandra smiled. "Anna, bring out the porcelain bowls."

"But, Madame—"

"Nancy is our friend, Anna," she said irritably. "Your caution annoys me at times. You keep everything hidden because you are afraid we shall be robbed. Why, you even distrust my grandson!"

The maid bit her lip but made no reply. She went over to a carved mahogany chest, unlocked it with a huge brass key, then removed porcelain bowls, enamel figurines, and other treasures.

"Do not forget the Footman!" Mrs. Alexandra ordered. "Perhaps Nancy can guess his secret."

Anna took out a rotund, lifelike figurine of porcelain. It stood about eight inches high and was unusual, but not as attractive as some of Mrs. Alexandra's other treasures.

"This and my Easter egg are my most prized possessions," the woman declared gaily. "The little statue looks like my own private footman at the palace. But also, he is special. Nancy, can you guess why?"

The girl shook her head, waiting expectantly.

"The figurine represents one of the most courageous of the court servants. My footman helped me escape during the Revolution. When I fled, I took this little object with me."

"Is it your jewel box, Mrs. Alexandra?"

"Yes. Is it not clever? I shall now reveal to you how it opens."

The woman reached for the small statue, but before she could show Nancy its secret, footsteps were heard on the staircase.

"Quick, Madame!" exclaimed Anna.

With amazing speed she snatched the Footman from Mrs. Alexandra and locked it in the chest, along with the other art treasures, then quickly hid the key under the rug.

"It is only Michael," Mrs. Alexandra said, recognizing her grandson's step.

"Nevertheless it is well that the treasures be kept out of sight," Anna insisted soberly.

Michael did not enter, but went on to his own room. Nancy, not wanting to meet him, thanked Mrs. Alexandra and said good-by. But she determined to come again soon to find out if the Footman were the jewel box mentioned in the nightingale's song.

As she was walking away from the house, Michael hurried after her. With flashing eyes, he confronted her.

"I heard you talking to my grandmother," he

stormed. "What's the idea of coming here? First you left me stranded on Star Island—"

"That was none of my doing," Nancy replied coldly. "I will say, though, that you deserved it."

"And then you deliberately got rid of my dog! One of the neighbors told me!"

"Your dog attacked the letter carrier. Rudy's been sent away for ten days' observation."

"If Rudy bit anyone, you probably made him do it!"

"How ridiculous!"

"I've caught on to the fact that you're trying to turn everyone against me," Michael went on, "especially Grandmother."

"That isn't true."

The unpleasant man edged closer to Nancy. "If you come here again, you'll get more than you bargained for!"

Before Nancy could voice an objection to his threat, he reentered the house, slamming the door behind him.

"I'll come here as frequently as I wish!" Nancy thought angrily. "At least as long as Mrs. Alexandra wants me! He is the one who should be kept from the house. He isn't bringing his grandmother any happiness, and I'm afraid she already has given him more money than she can afford."

For the first time in her life Nancy regretted having solved a mystery. By finding Prince Michael and restoring him to his grandmother,

Nancy feared she had only added to the unhappiness of the gracious former queen.

In returning home, she chose the familiar way, which led past Mr. Faber's shop. While still some distance from it, she noticed a man walking toward her with short, quick steps. He resembled David Dorrance. Though the man glanced at her, he passed with no sign of recognition.

"That must be Dorrance's double—the pickpocket!" Nancy thought excitedly.

She decided to follow him. The man did not pause until he reached the revolving doors of the Monroe office building.

Nancy quickened her pace. Suddenly the suspect halted. Half turning, but keeping his face slightly averted, he waved a white handkerchief.

"Wrong again!" Nancy thought in disgust, coming to a stop.

She recovered quickly from the unpleasant surprise and called Mr. Dorrance's name. Instead of replying, the man went inside.

Disappointed, Nancy retraced her way down the street. She had gone only fifty feet when she saw Mr. Faber running in her direction.

"I've been robbed! The thief went this way!"

CHAPTER XIII

Wanted—A Clue

THE antique dealer paused as he recognized Nancy. He was so excited it was difficult to understand what he was saying. She gathered, however, that a few minutes earlier a valuable gold-and-enamel penknife had disappeared from his show counter.

Mr. Faber cried, "Never can I replace it!"

"How was it taken?" Nancy asked quickly.

"Several customers were in my shop. A fellow asked to see the penknife. He took so long to decide I waited on the others."

Suddenly Mr. Faber pointed to a man who was coming out of a store across the street. "There he is now!"

The suspect resembled David Dorrance. This time Nancy had no doubt but that he was the long-sought pickpocket. Dorrance was some distance away in the Monroe Building.

"Mr. Faber, you must telephone the police!" Nancy advised. "I'll trail the thief!"

She tried to cross the street, but the traffic was heavy. Nancy found herself stranded in a center safety zone. The man identified by Faber was still in sight, but before she could reach him, he leaped into a taxi.

"Wait!" Nancy shouted to the driver.

He did not hear her, but the passenger turned his head. Upon seeing Nancy, he took a handkerchief from his pocket and waved it! Then the taxi sped on.

Nancy was completely bewildered. "Dorrance could not have spent more than a few seconds in the office building," she said to herself. "Why would he duck in and out so quickly? It doesn't make sense."

Many thoughts raced through her mind as she recrossed the street to Mr. Faber's shop. She was convinced that Dorrance had not gone from one place to the other.

"They were two different men!" she said. "But they both waved handkerchiefs and they look alike and wear the same kind of clothes."

Had the thief learned the method of identification that Dorrance used when seeing Nancy?

"That first man didn't give me the signal right away," she reflected. "So the second one must have been Dorrance."

A police car rushed up to Mr. Faber's shop.

The elderly man was so upset he was glad to have Nancy tell the story. She started it by asking the two officers to go with her at once to the Monroe Building.

"We may not be too late to nab the thief, if a hunch of mine is correct," she said.

They searched the building but without success. Discouraged, the three returned to the antique shop, where Faber described the stolen penknife.

"It was set with pearls," he concluded.

"We'll do what we can to locate it," one of the policemen promised. "That pickpocket is slippery. We've had that apartment house on Water Street watched constantly, but no one resembling the thief has turned up yet."

The following morning Nancy attended a final rehearsal of the fashion show. Early in the afternoon she arrived at the Woman's Club for the first performance. Katherine, pale and nervous, came in a few minutes later, accompanied by Helen Archer.

"Did you bring the hair ornament?" Nancy asked.

"Safe and sound." Helen laughed, producing the ruby-and-diamond piece.

With care Nancy put on the blue-flowered gown. The skirt with its short train swung gracefully to the floor.

"How do I look?" Nancy asked.

"Like the prettiest picture in a fashion book!" Helen complimented her.

Soon the dressing room was crowded with excited, chattering models. Everyone praised Nancy's costume. A few minutes before the show was scheduled to start, Bess and George came backstage.

"Nearly everyone of importance in River Heights is here," George told Nancy. "Even the Mayor!"

"Mrs. Alexandra came too with Anna," Bess added.

"She made the effort for Katherine's sake," Nancy said.

"Mrs. Alexandra like you very much too, Nancy," Katherine put in.

The orchestra had begun to play, and the models were told to take their places. One after another they stepped out from the wings.

"Now!" Katherine whispered, her voice tense.

The moment had arrived for her model to walk out upon the stage! Nancy made an effective entrance, carrying herself well. Each model had been greeted with a polite ripple of applause. Now the handclapping was loud and spontaneous.

Gracefully Nancy approached the carpeted steps which would carry her to the level of the audience. She saw Mrs. Alexandra's beaming face, and below her in the front row, Mr. Ellington, the artist. He nodded approvingly.

"He likes the gown!" she thought joyously.

Keeping perfect time to the music, Nancy moved down the first two steps. As she reached the third, there was a sudden sideways movement of the board beneath the carpet. Nancy tried to keep her balance. Instead she plunged headlong toward the floor!

As Nancy pitched forward, Mr. Ellington jumped up. Nancy fell directly into the young man's outstretched arms.

"Oh!" she cried, embarrassed.

There had been an audible gasp from the audience, and the music had ceased abruptly. Many feared the model had been injured.

"Are you hurt?" Mr. Ellington asked as he helped Nancy regain her balance.

Nancy shook her head, trying to recover her poise. She felt sick at heart, not so much for herself as for Katherine. Any chance of the young designer winning a prize was gone, she felt sure.

"Don't let this disturb you," Mr. Ellington whispered kindly. "It wasn't your fault!"

Thus encouraged, Nancy smiled bravely. The orchestra began to play again. She glided down the center aisle and back. During the intermission carpenters repaired the faulty step.

"Oh Katherine, I knew I would ruin your chances!" Nancy cried when she met the designer. "Why did I have to stumble?"

"It wasn't your fault," Helen interjected.

Nancy fell directly into the young man's arms

"No, indeed," echoed Katherine. "Tomorrow you make a grand entrance!"

Although everyone declared that the accident had been unavoidable, the three girls did not feel very cheerful. They brightened, however, when Mr. Ellington sought out Katherine to tell her that he considered her design the most original one entered in the show.

"If I were one of the judges, I'd vote to give you first prize," he declared warmly.

Katherine blushed and became flustered. He talked for a long while. It was obvious to Nancy that his interest was more than a professional one.

"What a grand couple they would make!" she remarked to Helen.

"Mr. Ellington is very charming," Helen agreed. "Isn't it a pity Michael couldn't—"

"Sh!" Nancy warned suddenly.

Mrs. Alexandra was approaching, followed by Anna. "You were charming, Nancy," the former queen said. "Will you have luncheon with me at one o'clock tomorrow? As you say in America, we have some unfinished business."

"Thank you, but I'm afraid I can't. I am due here before three for the afternoon showing."

"I shall see that you are not late."

Nancy was still hesitant about accepting the invitation. Her last meeting with Michael had been unpleasant, and she feared he might create a scene should he find her a guest in his home.

"Michael will not be there," Anna whispered.

"I'll be delighted to come, Mrs. Alexandra," Nancy accepted at once.

After the former queen and Anna had gone, Michael again became the topic of conversation. Katherine, who had rejoined the girls, admitted that the young man had called her several times.

"He annoy me with attentions I do not like! He send me flowers! He ask me for dates! Always I say No, but it does no good."

"I'd give anything if I never had traced him for Mrs. Alexandra," Nancy said soberly.

When she appeared at the woman's home the next day, the topic of Michael was studiously avoided. A delicious luncheon was served during which biscuits were passed in a quaint wooden basket with a royal crown on the handle.

At the close of the meal Mrs. Alexandra asked Anna to bring the Footman jewel box to her. Tenderly the former queen held the quaint porcelain and enamel figure.

"I shall now open it for you," she said to Nancy. "Can you guess how it is done?"

"By a secret spring?"

"Yes. First I press the little fellow here."

Mrs. Alexandra touched the Footman's left hand. To Nancy's amazement, the black coat of the figure loosened, enabling the woman to remove it. She pressed another spring and a panel slid open. Inside were a ruby ring, an unset emerald, a necklace of matched pearls, and two diamond bracelets.

"All that remain of my jewels," Mrs. Alexandra said. "Piece by piece I sold the others."

"These are exquisite," Nancy replied. "Did the box ever contain anything except jewelry?"

"No, it has always been used for that purpose. You are disappointed, perhaps?"

"I'm not disappointed, Mrs. Alexandra. I'll admit, though, that the little nightingale's words led me to believe this box might contain something else of importance.

"Katherine has told me the people of your country have many secrets," Nancy went on. "One of them is a process for making noncrackable enamel. I admit I wondered if the Footman might be hiding the lost formula."

Mrs. Alexandra tried to suppress a smile. "My dear," she said kindly, "I wonder if the song of the nightingale has not been misinterpreted. The words are so indistinct."

"Perhaps, but we know the song was added long after the Easter egg was made," Nancy remarked.

"Until Mr. Faber told you differently, I assumed that the nightingale was exactly as it had been created for me."

"You have no idea when the addition was made?"

"It must have been during the early days of the Revolution. I was away from the palace when the trouble started. There was such turmoil that I could not get back for some time."

"Then the song may have been added while you were away," Nancy suggested. "Perhaps some-one tried to provide you with an important clue —a clue meant for no other person. Who besides yourself had access to the Easter egg, Mrs. Alex-andra?"

"Only a few trusted servants in the palace."

"Who in your country was skillful at making music boxes?" Nancy asked eagerly.

"Conrad Nicholas," Mrs. Alexandra said, "the husband of Nada's sister. Nada was the nurse of my grandson Michael."

"Could she have borrowed the Easter egg?"

"Yes."

"Why, it all fits in beautifully!" Nancy ex-claimed. "Mrs. Alexandra, I'm convinced some jewel box contains a vital clue, and it must be this Footman. Maybe it holds a secret greater than all your jewels! The box may have another opening, perhaps in the legs of the Footman."

"But I have already examined the little statue from his head to the top of his boots! The secret, if there is one, has been cleverly hidden."

"Mrs. Alexandra, do you mind if I try?"

Smiling, the former queen placed the jewel box in Nancy's hands. With trembling fingers the young detective began to explore the porcelain and enamel figure inch by inch.

CHAPTER XIV

A Question of Honesty

ALTHOUGH Nancy carefully ran her fingers over the Footman figurine, pressing here and there, she did not discover a spring or release mechanism. The only opening appeared to be the one under the black coat.

"I can't find it." Sighing, Nancy returned the figurine to her hostess. "Someday, with your permission, I would like to try again."

"By all means."

A clock chimed the hour of two-thirty. Reminded that she should leave at once for the fashion show, Nancy hurried away.

A few minutes later, upon reaching the Woman's Club, she was surprised to see an excited crowd near the main entrance. A policeman had placed someone under arrest.

Approaching closer, Nancy observed that the suspect, who was arguing with the officer, closely resembled David Dorrance. At once the man turned and recognized her.

"Miss Drew, tell this policeman he's made a mistake!" he pleaded.

"I'm not sure—" she began.

"Sure, you recognize me! See!"

He gave the familiar white handkerchief signal. Nancy had but a moment to spare, because she was late now. She did not know what to say. As she hesitated, Dorrance added:

"I came here to see the show."

Nancy was convinced that he was the man who had come to her home. The policeman knew Nancy and asked her for a definite identification. She hesitated to answer, because she had not forgotten the double handkerchief episode on Main Street. Finally she told the officer she could not identify Dorrance as the wanted pickpocket.

"I don't believe this is the man you want. At least, he's not the one who stole Mr. Baum's wallet."

"Go on in, then," he told the man. "Sorry."

Dorrance would have lingered to chat with Nancy, but she had no time. She hastened to the dressing room and donned the Renaissance gown just as the orchestra began to play.

"I'll try to do better than yesterday," she said to Katherine when it was her turn on stage.

With perfect composure and the grace of a professional model, Nancy went through her simple routine. She returned to the wings amid thunderous applause.

"You were a sensation!" Helen exclaimed. "You and that gorgeous gown are the talk of the show!"

During a brief intermission Nancy wandered out into the audience. Before she got all the way down the center aisle, a woman close by uttered a piercing wail.

"My pocketbook! It's been stolen!"

Immediately the entire room was thrown into confusion. In the resulting excitement, Nancy spied David Dorrance slipping out the exit.

Forgetting her part in the show, Nancy sped after the fleeing man. When she reached the door, he was hurrying toward an alley.

"Wait!" she called.

The man turned, but did not pause. Nancy spied two little boys directly ahead and shouted:

"Stop that man! Don't let him get away!"

The boys attempted to block his path, but he shoved them away angrily. Nancy ran after him as fast as she could. The long evening gown impeded her progress.

Nevertheless, she began to gain on the thief. At the end of the alley, the man darted around a corner. He saw a long coil of barbed wire lying on the ground. Seizing it, he threw it in such a way that Nancy could not fail to run against the sharp barbs.

Unsuspecting, she ran straight into the wire. Her gown caught in a dozen places, tearing badly. Aghast, she halted.

"Oh, this beautiful gown!" she thought, seeing that it had been torn beyond repair. "I've ruined Katherine's chances completely!"

Out of breath and disheveled, Nancy returned to the clubhouse. It was time for the second half of the fashion show to begin.

Suddenly in the throng Nancy saw David Dorrance!

"Why, Miss Drew, what has happened to you?" he asked, walking over to her.

The man was perfectly composed. There was no indication, either in his breathing or the color of his face, that he had been running.

"I mistook him again for the pickpocket!" Nancy thought, chagrined.

"Just a little accident," she replied, and dashed to the dressing room. A sudden thought came to her.

"It's uncanny that Dorrance and the thief are so often in the same place! I'm going to talk to the police about it!"

Nancy found Katherine and Helen waiting for her. When they saw the ruined gown, they were dismayed.

"Oh, Nancy, how did it happen?" Helen managed to say at last.

Nancy told about pursuing the pickpocket. "I

ought to stick to sleuthing and give up trying to model in fashion shows," she concluded grimly. "The two certainly don't mix."

"What are we to do?" Helen asked, sinking into a chair. "The dress can't be mended."

"I don't appear in the show again until tomorrow afternoon. That gives us twenty-four hours. Couldn't you duplicate the dress, Katherine? You had a good bit of material left over."

"In so short time! No, no."

"Maybe part of it could be saved," Nancy added. "The sleeves are in perfect condition."

"And so is all the back except the train," Helen encouraged her. "Couldn't you just make a new front and replace the train, Katherine?"

"I could sew all night, if necessary," Nancy offered.

The designer made a hasty examination of the gown. A minute later her eyes lighted up. "I can do it!"

The girls hastened to Katherine's shop. For two hours they sewed steadily. By then it was evident that the work could be finished in time.

"We go home now and rest," Katherine urged. "I finish the dress tomorrow."

The young designer locked the shop, and the three girls walked down the street. At the corner Nancy left the others to go to police headquarters. There she reported her suspicions regarding Dorrance and his double.

"It seems strange to me that those two men should always be in the same place at the same time," she said to Chief McGinnis.

The officer gave her a friendly smile. "Do you think they are brothers—twins maybe?" he asked.

"They look enough alike," Nancy replied. "At first I thought only one was a thief, but now I'm wondering whether Dorrance is really innocent."

"I'm glad you've told me this," said the chief. "As you know, my men haven't been able to catch that pickpocket, or solve the mystery of the rash of thefts going on in River Heights. You've given us a new clue."

When Nancy arrived home she found an urgent telephone message awaiting her from Anna. It requested her to come to the Alexandra house as soon as possible.

"Of course I'll go," Nancy said to Hannah Gruen, "but I hate to meet Michael."

Nancy thought it best to go to the rear entrance and parked on a back street. Anna met her at the door, and they conversed in the kitchen.

"Is Mrs. Alexandra ill?" Nancy inquired anxiously. "Your note—"

"She is sick here." Anna indicated the region of her heart. "Sick because of Michael."

"What has he done now, Anna?"

"I learned something dreadful only yesterday. Madame Marie has given him many valuables to sell."

"I knew Mrs. Alexandra had sent him once to Mr. Faber."

"Not once, but many times. And he has gone to other shops. The prices paid have not been high. Much too low for their value."

"How dreadful!" said Nancy.

"Something is wrong," Anna declared. "I say it is time to ask questions of Michael. But Madame Marie will not do it!"

"Doesn't he bring back signed receipts?"

"He gives her nothing, except a few dollars."

Nancy's mind was working fast. "Anna, can you give me a list of the pieces Mrs. Alexandra has sold through Michael? Also the amounts he gave her?"

"I have it all here," the woman declared.

"Then I'll check the items at once with the shopkeepers," Nancy promised.

At that moment a door slammed and Michael's whistle was heard in the hall.

"I must go quickly before he sees me," Nancy whispered, opening the screen door.

She slipped through the garden to the back street, and drove at once to Mr. Faber's shop. The antique dealer was looking out the front door.

"Oh, Mr. Faber," she greeted him, running up, "may I talk with you a moment?"

"Certainly," he replied, noting her agitation. "Is something wrong?"

"I don't know," Nancy replied. "Are you willing to tell me how much you paid Michael for the ring he sold to you?"

"Three hundred dollars. It would have bought more if he had been willing to wait for me to find a buyer. He insisted Madame Alexandra had to have cash at once."

Nancy inspected the sales list she had brought with her. According to Anna's notation, Michael had given his grandmother only one hundred dollars for the ring. Apparently he had kept the remaining money.

"Mr. Faber, I'm sorry to say this, but I think Michael is dishonest. Please examine this list."

The antique dealer frowned as he read the amounts paid by various shopkeepers for other treasures.

"These objects are worth far more than Madame Alexandra received," he said. "Come into the shop while I telephone."

His anger aroused, Mr. Faber called one of the firms listed. He learned that a jade and enamel vase had been sold for a large amount, but Michael had given his grandmother only a small percentage of the money received. Another dealer reported he had paid the young man five hundred dollars for an antique tapestry. Yet only one-fifth of this had been turned over to Mrs. Alexandra!

"Michael has cheated his grandmother!" Mr. Faber exclaimed.

"It's just possible Mrs. Alexandra intended

Michael to have the rest as spending money, but did not wish to tell Anna," Nancy suggested.

"It will kill Madame Alexandra if she finds out that her grandson is a common thief," Mr. Faber declared.

"We must do nothing until we are sure," said Nancy with determination.

It was dark when Nancy finally left the antique shop. She reached her own street and turned into the Drew driveway. The windows of the house were dark.

"Hannah must be in the basement and forgot to turn on the first-floor lights," Nancy thought as she parked and walked toward the side door.

Suddenly, from behind some tall bushes, two men arose. Stocking masks hid their faces.

"All right!" muttered one of them.

Nancy started to scream, but a hand was clapped over her mouth, and she was held in a grip of steel.

CHAPTER XV

A Threat

As Nancy struggled vainly to free herself, one of the men spoke. His voice sounded disguised.

"Nancy Drew, I'm warning you that if you don't do as we tell you, you'll be sorry, and your father sorrier. You've got to mind your own business!"

Nancy squirmed sideways, trying to see her captors. The men's masks made it impossible to distinguish their features.

The taller of the two gave her a rough shake. "Will you promise?"

"Promise what?" Nancy mumbled as the hand on her mouth was lifted slightly.

"Stop trying to be a detective!"

"Are you afraid I'll have you arrested?" Nancy countered.

An automobile was coming down the street, its headlights cutting a path along the dark pavement. The engine had a familiar sound. Her father's car! Nancy took heart. She must keep on sparring for time until he turned in.

She struggled to break free. "Take your hands off me!" she mumbled but the men paid no attention. They held on tighter and once more made their demand.

The car, which had been approaching slowly, turned into the Drew driveway. Nancy gave a quick jerk, freeing her mouth for a second.

"Help! Help!" she shouted.

The man who held her gave the girl a sudden push which sent her reeling into the steps of the side porch.

"Come on!" he snapped to his companion. "We'd better get out of here!"

Crouching low, they ran along the hedge, and disappeared into the protecting shadows of the garden next door.

Carson Drew leaped from his car and hurried to Nancy's side. She fell into his arms, exhausted by the encounter.

"Why did you scream?" he demanded anxiously.

"Two men—" She pointed to where they had gone. "Oh, Dad, if you hadn't come, I don't know what would have happened."

Breathlessly Nancy told him how his timely arrival had saved her from further threats. She and her father quickly ran in the direction the men had taken and searched in the neighbor's garden, but the strangers had disappeared.

"Did you recognize either of them, Nancy? How were they dressed?"

"They wore stocking masks. The build of one of the men resembled that of David Dorrance and his double."

"The thief is afraid you're getting too hot on his trail," Mr. Drew said thoughtfully.

Nancy told of her suspicions and of her report to the police.

"I'm glad you told the chief," he replied. "And hereafter, let them track down the pickpocket. You'll only be inviting danger if you continue to trail him. Next time I might not be around to save you!" he added affectionately, and took her hand as he led her back to their home.

"I've been hoping," Nancy said, "to recover the money for the Boys Club and your stolen papers."

"The thief probably has spent the money by this time," Mr. Drew replied. "Don't worry any more about my wallet. Buy me another for my birthday!"

As they sat at dinner a little later, she observed that her father looked worried.

"Nancy," he said quietly, "I wish you would stop taking so much interest in Mrs. Alexandra."

"Why, Dad"—Nancy stared at her father in dismay—"I can't abandon the dear lady to Michael's clutches! Only today I learned that he has been robbing her of rather large sums of money. Wait until you see this paper!" she added, getting the slip from her purse.

Mr. Drew inspected the sales notations obtained through Anna and Mr. Faber.

"You don't expect Mrs. Alexandra to believe that her grandson is a thief?" he asked.

"No, and I don't intend to tell her until I have more proof."

"Don't do anything until I've had time to consider the legal angle," her father advised.

"I'll wait," Nancy promised. "Telling the poor woman the truth will probably end our friendship, anyway."

As she spoke, the telephone rang. Mrs. Gruen answered it, and then reported that the call was for Nancy.

"I think it's Helen Archer," the housekeeper said.

Fearing that there might be some new difficulty regarding the torn gown, Nancy ran to talk to her friend.

"For once I haven't a scrap of bad news to report," Helen assured her. "Mr. Ellington phoned and wants us to organize a hayride. Of course he'll be Katherine's partner."

"Tonight?"

"No, tomorrow after the evening performance. He suggests we go to the Red Lion Inn for supper and dancing."

"A hayride would be fun!" Nancy exclaimed. "Tell me more about it."

"Mr. Ellington is sure Katherine is going to win the grand prize at the fashion show, so he wants to give a party for her. Unfortunately he can't join us until we reach the inn," Helen explained. "He has a business appointment in Harbortown."

For some time the two girls discussed plans for the hayride, working out every detail. A window not far from where Nancy sat was open, and the curtains fluttered in the breeze, just enough for anyone outside to look in. A man was crouching below, listening to the telephone conversation. Nancy had her back turned, and did not notice.

"We'll have a grand time tomorrow night," she declared before hanging up. "Especially if Katherine wins the big prize! And I'm sure she will!"

Since Nancy wanted to appear fresh for the next day's fashion show, she went to bed early. For a long while she tossed on her pillow, thinking of the puzzles which confronted her. Of them all, she was still particularly intrigued by the little nightingale's words, "clue in jewel box."

"The jewel box must be the Footman," she thought over and over. "The queen mother's family and trusted servants knew it was the one holding her most valuable pieces."

Nancy felt that the revelation of the secret might in some way make up to Mrs. Alexandra for the disgraceful behavior of the prince.

"That little Footman must have another opening," she reflected.

Try as she would, Nancy could think of no way to open it. Morning did not bring any solution to the vexing problem. It continued to plague Nancy throughout the day, even as she went through her afternoon routine at the fashion show. Then, just as she left the building, an idea flashed into her mind.

"That may be it!" Nancy thought excitedly. "I must go to Mrs. Alexandra's home at once. I only hope I won't find Michael there!"

CHAPTER XVI

The Prize Winner

CURTAINS were closed at the Alexandra home, but Anna opened the front door almost as soon as Nancy rang the bell.

"Madame is very low in spirit," the woman whispered and sighed. "It is Michael! This morning he asked her to give him a very valuable bracelet to sell."

"She didn't do it?"

"Not yet, but she is considering it very seriously. Oh, can you not do something to save what remains of my good lady's fortune?"

"I hope to, Anna. I have proof that Michael kept most of the money he received from dealers."

"She will never believe it."

"Probably not," Nancy said. "And anyway, there's a legal angle. Being related, he could say she gave it to him. My father is going to see about that. But I came here for another reason. Michael isn't at home, is he?"

"He is with his grandmother now."

"Then I will leave and come another time."

"No, wait," the woman urged. "Hide in this closet. I will send Michael out."

Nancy secreted herself in the hall closet as instructed. Soon she heard the young man arguing loudly with Anna.

"You always want me to go on errands for you!" he complained. "I'm a prince and you're supposed to wait on me."

An outside door slammed and Nancy knew that Michael had gone. A few moments later Anna opened the closet door.

"I have announced to Madame that you are here," she told Nancy. "She will see you now."

Knowing that Michael would not be gone long, Nancy did not waste words as she explained to Mrs. Alexandra that she would like to try once more to find another opening in the Footman jewel box.

"I have an idea that I think may work," she added earnestly.

Mrs. Alexandra smiled and asked Anna to bring the precious statue. As Nancy took it, she said:

"When I was a little girl my grandmother gave me a very old music box that had belonged to her. It had a secret drawer in it, which opened in a peculiar fashion."

Her fingers explored the figurine. "If only it will work—"

With increasing interest the two women watched Nancy skillfully manipulate the jewel box. Suddenly Mrs. Alexandra gave a cry of delight.

"My Footman's boot! It is coming off!"

Nancy nodded. Her hunch had been correct!

"But there is nothing in the foot," Mrs. Alexandra added, disappointed.

Nancy peered into the tiny boot. Thrusting her little finger into it, she loosened a folded piece of paper.

"This must be the clue that the nightingale tried to tell us!" she exclaimed.

Nancy longed to look at the paper, but instead politely handed it to the former queen. Mrs. Alexandra pondered a long time over the words scrawled on the paper. Nancy began to doubt that the woman would ever reveal the contents. Finally she spoke.

"Anna," she requested, "please leave us alone for a few minutes."

After Anna had left, Madame Alexandra gave Nancy the paper. The young detective was unable to read the words. They were in a foreign language. The woman, her voice vibrant with excitement, translated them in a whisper.

"This information is amazing!" Nancy exclaimed.

"Sh!" the woman warned. "Do not speak aloud of the great secret. No one must know of it yet—not even Anna."

"But neither you nor I can carry out the instructions on this paper," said Nancy.

"You must ask some fine young man to help you," Madame Alexandra advised.

"My friend Ned is very capable, and he's just the person to help me."

From the window Nancy saw Michael coming back with a package.

"I must go now," she said hurriedly.

Anna had met the young man on the front walk, and engaged him in conversation until Nancy could leave by the rear door. He was talking loudly.

"I'm too busy to be running to the store for you," he said crossly. "And you don't need all this stuff, anyway. I won't be here to dinner tonight, and maybe not all night, either!"

Without lingering to hear more, Nancy headed home in a state of thoughtfulness. When Hannah Gruen tried to learn the reason for her faraway expression, Nancy merely smiled and said, "Tomorrow I expect to solve a great mystery."

Later, at the Woman's Club, Nancy's dreamy mood persisted. It lent a warm glow to her skin. Helen Archer complimented her friend. "I've never seen you look prettier."

"I feel as if I were walking in a dream," Nancy murmured. "Am I really in this fashion show?"

"There is your cue now!" Helen replied.

Nancy glided gracefully down the carpeted stairway, treading as lightly as if on air. She pivoted, displaying the Renaissance gown to the best advantage. The lovely tiara-like headdress sparkled under the lights, adding the final touch to the exquisite costume. When Nancy returned to the wings, thunderous applause followed.

"You were terrific!" Helen exclaimed.

Katherine praised Nancy, too, but she did not feel confident that the Renaissance gown would win the grand prize. Other costumes had received much attention. She was certain that a white satin evening dress, created by a professional designer, Wilbur de Wolf, might be named by the judges.

Soon it was time for the all-important decisions to be announced. An expectant hush fell over the audience. Nancy joined the other models crowding into the wings.

One of the judges made a little speech, praising all who had helped with the show. "And now, ladies and gentlemen," he said in conclusion, "I take great pleasure in awarding the prizes."

Quickly he presented trophies for the sport and daytime dresses.

"And now, will Mr. Wilbur de Wolf please come forward. His design, modeled by—"

Nancy heard no more. Katherine had grabbed her hand, and a little sob of disappointment had escaped from the girl. She started to walk away, but was hemmed in by the crowd of people in the wings.

When the applause died down, the voice of the judge boomed out again. "The grand prize—and may I say the vote of the committee was unanimous—goes to Miss Katherine Kovna, designer of the Renaissance gown modeled by Miss Nancy Drew."

Further words were drowned by the loud applause. Katherine, blinded by tears, hesitated. Quickly she dried her eyes and then appeared on the stage with Nancy. Katherine was so overcome with happiness she could only say, "Thank you."

Nancy graciously acknowledged the honor paid to the young designer and her creation. Flashbulbs went off as photographers snapped pictures, and reporters pressed for statements.

"I never was so happy in my life!" Katherine declared when at last the excitement was over.

Nancy quickly changed into a sports outfit, which could be worn on the hayride.

"I hope Richard meet us at the inn on time," Katherine remarked wistfully. "I do want him to know at once who won the big prize."

After Nancy and Ned had returned the precious headdress to Madame Alexandra, the group of young people going to the supper and dance met at the ferry and crossed the river. A hayrack pulled by two large gray horses awaited them on the opposite shore. Amid shouts of laughter the group scrambled onto it.

Jim Archer relieved the farmer of the reins, and the horses started off. Bess began to sing a familiar song. The others joined in.

"Why so quiet, Nancy?" Ned asked when he noticed she was not singing.

"Oh, just thinking," she replied. "Ned, will you do me a favor?"

"Just name it, and it's done."

"I'll tell you about it later."

An hour later Jim brought the hayrack safely into the parking lot of the Red Lion Inn. One by one the young people climbed out, brushing wisps of hay from their clothing.

"We're sights, but it's worth it!" George laughed as she straightened her short, wind-blown hair. "And I'm hungry!"

"Look who's here!" said Bess, nudging Nancy.

Michael and a tall young man whose face they could not see quickly crossed the parking lot and entered the restaurant. Nancy's heart began to beat excitedly. Michael's companion had bushy hair and wore a dark jacket!

"He's the man who stole the jeweled ornament from me!" she thought. "I'm sure of it!"

Quietly she told the others. "Seeing them together makes me think that Michael was behind the theft," she said.

"Are you going to call the police?" Bess asked.

"Not now," Nancy replied. "We may learn something by watching the two of them."

The young people trooped into the old inn. It was a long, brick building with a stone chimney at each end. The candle-lighted interior had been restored with its Colonial furnishings.

"What a delightful place for a party!" said Katherine. "Now we find Richard."

Ned learned from the headwaiter that the artist had not arrived yet.

"That's odd," said Nancy. "We're late too."

"Maybe he changed his plans at the last minute," Helen suggested a while later.

Katherine was quiet, and the others realized that she was very much embarrassed. Twice Michael had come to the table and asked her to dance. She not only had refused, but changed seats to be near Nancy.

"I worry about Richard," she said.

"If I only knew his address, I could telephone," Nancy said thoughtfully.

Katherine volunteered the information that Mr. Ellington lived at an apartment house known as the Warrington Arms. She and Nancy left the room and looked for a booth in the hall. A friend who lived with him answered.

"No, Mr. Ellington is not here," he told Nancy. "About an hour ago he called from Harbortown, saying he planned to go directly to the Red Lion Inn."

Thanking the man for the information, Nancy hung up and turned to face her friend.

"He should have been here long ago," she said, growing more alarmed. "Harbortown is only a mile from here."

"What happened to him?" cried Katherine. "Maybe his car go off road—an accident!"

"I was thinking the same thing," Nancy replied quietly. "It seems to me that we should call the police."

CHAPTER XVII

Telephone Tip

NANCY immediately telephoned the police department. No accidents had been reported within the past hour, and no one of Richard Ellington's description had been reported in trouble.

"I guess we worried unnecessarily," Nancy thought in relief. "But it's strange that he should be delayed so long."

As she opened the door of the booth, Nancy was surprised to find that Katherine had gone. Instantly she knew why. Michael was walking in Nancy's direction. She would have passed him with only a cold nod if he had not blocked her path.

"Miss Drew, may I say something to you?" he asked in a wheedling tone.

Nancy was surprised at the young man's change of attitude toward her. What did his sudden friendly overture mean?

"I want to apologize for the way I've acted," he went on. "I said some things I didn't mean."

"I'll accept your apology," Nancy replied.

"We ought to be good friends. Grandmother wants it that way."

"Yes, I guess she does," Nancy said. After a pause she added, "Suppose I come to the house tomorrow to tea. Will you be there?"

"Tomorrow? Uh—no—yes. I had some business to attend to, but I'll put it off."

Nancy felt sure the man had some ulterior motive for being so polite and friendly.

"Grandmother thinks I'm tops now," Michael went on. "She'll keep on thinking that if Anna will just mind her own business. The old busybody keeps telling Grandmother not to give me money. I have to baby Anna along all the time. Why don't you put in a good word for me?"

Nancy smiled, realizing now why the man had adopted such a cordial attitude.

"So you think I have influence with Anna?" she asked.

"Sure. Whatever you say goes with her. How about it?"

"We'll see," Nancy replied. "Be sure to be at home tomorrow afternoon. By the way, who was the man with you?"

Michael showed surprise at the question but answered, "I don't know. I picked him up a little way from here."

Before Michael could query Nancy about her interest in the stranger, she moved on to rejoin her friends.

Katherine Kovna and everyone else was relieved to hear that Mr. Ellington had not been in an accident.

The young dress designer's evening, however, was spoiled. The others were very kind to her, and the boys saw to it that she danced a great deal. While Nancy and Ned were dancing together, he asked what she thought of Richard Ellington not making an appearance.

"I'm really worried that something has happened to him," she replied. "He's too much of a gentleman not to have sent word."

"Well, if he wasn't in an accident, what else would have delayed him?" Ned persisted.

"Lots of things. Thieves could have waylaid him, knocked him out, and stolen his car."

"Then let's get out of here and go look for him," Ned suggested.

He was glad of an excuse to walk in the moonlight with Nancy. As they followed the road that wound in and out along the river, Ned felt only the romance of the evening.

But Nancy's thoughts kept reverting to the mystery. It was an eerie night. Now and then clouds would obscure the moon, causing grotesque shadows to flicker across their path.

"Ned, what was that?" Nancy stopped short,

gripping his arm. "I saw a figure hiding behind that giant pine tree," she whispered. "We're being followed."

"Why should anyone follow us? Come on," he urged. "You want to find Ellington, don't you?"

Somewhat dubiously, Nancy allowed herself to be led on down the road. She kept her gaze fastened on the line of trees. Suddenly the moving shadow appeared again.

"Ned, I'm sure we're being spied upon!"

The boy started toward the trees, but Nancy pulled him back.

"We're in danger," she cautioned. "I can't explain more now, but we must go right back."

Quickly she turned and began to run, Ned at her heels. Not until she was within the rays of light from the inn did she slow down to a walk.

"Now tell me what's going on," Ned panted.

"Something of tremendous importance is at stake. I don't trust Michael, and I feel his being here tonight is to establish an alibi. I have a plan that I was going to carry out tomorrow, but I think I should do so tonight."

"The one you wanted me to help you with?"

"Yes. Get Jim and wait here for me. I'll locate our victim!" she replied tensely.

Scarcely had Ned vanished into the inn when Nancy saw a tall man coming hurriedly along the road. He was Michael's companion. Quickly she ducked behind a bush.

"He must be the one who followed Ned and me," she thought.

The man passed close to where she crouched. Without noticing her, he entered the inn.

"I'll trail him!" Nancy determined.

As she entered the hallway of the inn, she saw him go into the dining room. Nancy was about to follow when from a half-closed telephone booth she recognized a familiar voice.

"Everything's going as planned," Michael said in a mocking tone. "Yes, I'm with Nancy Drew now. How's my dear grandma? Ha! Ha!"

Nancy moved closer, but she heard no more. Michael lowered his voice, and a moment later came from the booth.

"Now what was the significance of that conversation?" the bewildered girl asked herself. "Michael couldn't have been talking to Anna. He's up to something!"

With no suspicion that he was being observed, Michael started to return to the dining room. Quickly Nancy walked up to him.

"Wouldn't you like to join some of us in the garden?" she asked sweetly.

The young man looked surprised but accepted the invitation. Nancy suggested he wait for her by a little pool. He went outside just as Ned returned with Helen and Jim.

"How would you like to expose an impostor?" Nancy whispered.

"What!" said the three in unison.

"Anything you say," Jim agreed.

"I'm convinced that the man known as Michael Alexandra is not a prince," Nancy whispered tensely.

"What do you want us to do?" asked Jim.

"How are you at kidnapping?"

"Expert." Ned grinned.

"It must be a neat, noiseless job. We'll all walk down to the pool, where Michael is waiting. When I give the signal, overpower him and I'll tell you what to do."

"Leave it to us!" Ned replied.

The young people wandered into the garden. They paused at the pool, forming a circle about the unsuspecting Michael. Then, at a signal from Nancy, Jim and Ned closed in from the rear.

Before the captive could make a sound, they had covered his mouth. Lifting him bodily they carried him behind some bushes and put him down. No one would be apt to notice them in that spot, but there was enough light from a nearby lamp for them to see. Nancy spoke up quickly.

"If you don't yell for help, we'll allow you to talk," she told him.

Ned removed his hand from the young man's mouth.

"What's the idea?" Michael demanded. "You can't treat me like this! I'm a prince—"

"How can you prove it?" Nancy demanded.

"With the letter and photograph. You took them to Grandmother yourself!"

"I gave her certain proofs—yes. But how do I know where you obtained them? They may have belonged to another person."

"That's a lie," Michael mumbled, struggling hard to break away from Ned and Jim.

Nancy resumed coolly, "I know that you have been robbing Mrs. Alexandra."

"You can't prove a thing! You're bluffing! Grandmother is satisfied that I am the lost prince."

"If you're the missing Michael, you can prove your identity right now," Nancy retorted.

"I don't know what you're talking about," he protested savagely.

"You will in a moment." Nancy smiled as she turned to Ned and Jim. "Boys," she said, "please remove this man's shoes and socks."

"What's the big idea?" Michael protested furiously. "You can't take off my shoes!"

"Oh, can't we?" mocked Jim. "Just watch us!"

While their captive struggled and fought, he and Ned stripped off the shoes and socks.

"I wish we had a flashlight," Nancy commented.

"Here's one in the prince's pocket," Ned said sarcastically. He handed it to her.

To the surprise of the young people Nancy flashed the light directly on the soles of Michael's bare feet.

"You are an impostor!" Nancy exclaimed

"Just as I thought!" she exclaimed. "You are not Mrs. Alexandra's long-lost grandson! You are an impostor!"

"That's not true," the young man whined. "Why are you looking at my feet?"

"If you actually were Michael Alexandra, you would know the answer without asking!"

"You're just trying to cheat me out of my inheritance."

Nancy was stern as she faced the captive. "You'll never obtain another penny from Mrs. Alexandra! Your little game has ended."

Michael stared sullenly at the group.

"Okay, I'll admit I'm not Michael Alexandra."

"Where did you obtain your so-called credentials?" Nancy asked sharply. "I mean the letter and picture and toy?"

"Found 'em on a train seat coming into River Heights."

"Then the real Prince Michael may be somewhere near here!" Nancy exclaimed. She asked the impostor, "Where is he?"

CHAPTER XVIII

Cornering a Thief

"I DON'T know who the guy is, or where he went," the man insisted sullenly.

"Did you see him?" Nancy persisted. "What did he look like?"

Michael shrugged. "Don't remember."

"What's your real name?" Nancy asked.

Michael did not reply. Suspecting that the police would be summoned, he sat down on the ground, waiting for a chance to escape.

Nancy went into the inn and telephoned headquarters. Then she spoke to the others at the table, asking two of the young men to locate Michael's companion. He could not be found anywhere, and Nancy assumed he had learned about what was going on and had left. A police car soon arrived and took away the prisoner.

"Let's go inside," Helen said. "Then you can

tell us, Nancy, how you found out about the mark that will identify the lost prince."

"I'll tell you about it later," the young detective replied. "In this public place someone might overhear me."

Nancy followed the others toward the inn. After going a short distance she paused.

"Something else wrong?" Ned inquired.

"I can't help being worried about Mrs. Alexandra and Anna," she confessed, frowning.

"With the impostor in the hands of the police," Ned answered, "they should be safe."

"That's the point, Ned. The prisoner is a clever thief, and he may have accomplices."

"But his pals wouldn't be likely to make trouble for Mrs. Alexandra without a go-ahead from him."

"I'm not so sure of that. He's the one we know so he'd have to establish an alibi. Ned, I heard him talking on the phone a while ago."

"What did he say?"

" 'Everything's fine. I'm with Nancy Drew now. How's my dear grandma?' He asked that mockingly, almost as if he knew she might be in trouble."

"Do you think any of his pals are at the Alexandra house tonight?"

"That's just what I'm afraid of, Ned. When I learned what the clue in the jewel box was, I advised Mrs. Alexandra not to give Michael any more jewels or art objects to sell. If she acted on my suggestion, then he probably realized his little game was nearing an end."

"And figured he had to clean up fast," Ned stated.

Nancy nodded in reply. "He may have arranged for his pals to rob the house tonight. I overheard Michael tell Anna he probably wouldn't be home. When I asked him if he'd be there tomorrow, he seemed uncertain at first."

"I see what you mean about establishing an alibi!" Ned exclaimed. "Say, his pals may be robbing Mrs. Alexandra at this very minute!"

"Let's go to her house!"

"I'll ask Jim to come with us," Ned said.

Jim was more than willing to accompany the couple, and Katherine insisted upon going along. They found an empty taxi parked near the inn.

"Take us to the ferry right away!" Ned urged the driver.

"If we miss the next boat, there won't be another along for half an hour," Jim added, glancing at his watch.

Ten minutes later the taxi arrived at the dock. An instant before the gates were lowered, the cab was driven aboard. The ride across the river took its usual time, but to Nancy it seemed hours before the boat docked.

"Now to 47 Downey Street!" she urged the driver as the taxi rolled off the ramp.

The car sped through the streets, drawing up at last before the darkened house.

Jim paid the driver, and the young people went up the walk. Ned rang the doorbell but no response came from within the house. Again he pressed the button, holding his finger on it a long while.

"That's enough to wake anybody," he declared.

"I'm going inside," said Nancy. "I wonder if all the doors are locked."

"This one is," Jim reported, testing the knob.

The young people circled the house and tried the rear door. It too was locked, but Ned scrambled up a trellis to a window. The sash raised without difficulty. Ned crawled through and unlocked the back door.

"The house is certainly quiet," he reported in a whisper. "If the neighbors see us, they may report us as burglars."

"We can explain why we're here," Nancy replied, switching on lights as she walked through to the living room.

When the young people reached it, they were appalled by the sight before them. The expensive tapestries had been stripped from the walls. Many of the silk chair coverings had been slashed. All the art objects were missing.

"The house has been ransacked!" Nancy cried. "What has become of Mrs. Alexandra and

Anna?" Katherine cried, picking up a torn white apron.

"I'll look upstairs," said Nancy.

She started up the dark stairway, calling the names of the women. There was no answer.

Jim and Ned followed close behind her, groping for an electric switch.

"There must be one here somewhere," Nancy murmured, inching her way along the upper hall.

The next instant she stumbled over a body lying on the carpet.

"Ned! Jim!" she called, bending over the form.

Just as Nancy shouted that she had found someone lying on the floor, Ned's groping fingers located the electric switch at the top of the stairs. He pressed the button.

Recognizing the motionless figure, Nancy gasped, "It's Anna! She's bound and gagged!"

Katherine raced up the stairs. With a penknife Ned severed the cords, while Nancy removed the handkerchief from the woman's mouth. But she showed no sign of regaining consciousness.

Leaving the others to look after Anna, she hurried into Mrs. Alexandra's bedroom. Her worst fears were confirmed. The woman lay helpless on the bed. Her hands and feet were tightly bound, and a cloth had been stuffed into her mouth. Nancy removed the gag.

"Mrs. Alexandra, speak to me!" she pleaded.

The woman's eyelids fluttered open and then closed again. She lapsed into unconsciousness.

"We'd better call a doctor," Nancy said as Ned quickly cut the leg and arm cords.

Jim appeared in the doorway, carrying Anna. Carefully he laid her on the bed beside her mistress.

Nancy ran downstairs. Fortunately the telephone wire had not been cut, and she was able to summon a doctor. He arrived ten minutes later. The physician examined Anna briefly but spent a much longer time with Mrs. Alexandra.

"She's in serious condition," he said soberly. "I advise hospital care. I will make the necessary arrangements now."

While the physician made a telephone call, Nancy asked Jim to summon the police. She and Katherine remained with Mrs. Alexandra and Anna, while Ned looked through the house. Nancy quickly searched the bedroom for the chest containing the Footman jewel case. It was gone! Presently the doctor came back upstairs. "The ambulance will be here soon," he reported, pulling a chair to the bedside.

Nancy left the room and went to inspect the house. Almost everything of value except heavy pieces of furniture had been stolen. The Easter egg, a pair of gold candlesticks, the silverware—all articles that Mrs. Alexandra treasured.

"She will never survive this blow," Nancy said to Ned. "How can we tell her the truth?"

"Maybe the police can get some of the things back," he replied hopefully.

Within a few minutes a car arrived from headquarters. Nancy was able to give the officers a detailed description of nearly every object which had been stolen from the house.

"Any idea who committed the crime?" one of the policemen asked her.

"Yes, I have!" she answered. "The theft probably was engineered by the man who was arrested tonight on the other side of the river. I don't know his real name—he wouldn't tell me. He has been living here, posing as a relative and robbing Mrs. Alexandra."

"Then the actual robbery must have been done by one or more of his pals," the officer declared. "Mrs. Alexandra hasn't talked?"

"No, neither she nor her maid has been able to say a word."

"We may get something out of them after they recover from shock," the policeman said. "In the meantime, we'll talk to the prisoner. Maybe he'll reveal the identity of his accomplices."

Soon after the police had completed their inspection of the house, the ambulance arrived. Nancy and Katherine rode to the hospital with the patients. Nancy was given permission to remain in Mrs. Alexandra's room.

"I want to be here when she recovers consciousness," Nancy had explained to the nurse. "She may reveal something that will help the police make an arrest."

Katherine, meanwhile, had taken up her post in another room beside Anna's bed. Now and then she and Nancy would meet in the hall to hold whispered consultations.

"Anna—she spoke a little while ago," Katherine reported at one of the sessions.

"What did she say?" Nancy asked eagerly.

"She keep mumbling about a stolen jewel box."

"Then she must know what happened. Katherine, at the next opportunity try to get her to describe the man who bound her."

"I learn what I can," the girl promised.

Nancy returned to Mrs. Alexandra's bedside. A moment later the nurse excused herself to get some medication from another part of the hospital. The sound of the closing door seemed to arouse the patient from her long stupor. She opened her eyes, staring at Nancy without recognition.

"Do not strike me! I will tell you where my money is hidden!"

"Mrs. Alexandra, you're safe now," Nancy said soothingly. "Don't you know me? I am Nancy Drew."

Mrs. Alexandra relaxed slightly. She reached for the girl's hand and clung tightly to it.

"My jewels—" she whispered.

"Now don't worry about anything," Nancy comforted the woman.

With a deep sigh the former queen closed her eyes again.

"Mrs. Alexandra," Nancy said, fearing that the victim would lapse into a stupor once more, "did you see the man who tied you up?"

"I was upstairs alone when he came into the room," Mrs. Alexandra replied, speaking with great difficulty. "The man was thin, of medium height, and wore a black mask. That's all I remember."

Before Nancy could ask another question, Katherine appeared in the doorway. She motioned to the young detective to come out into the hall.

"Anna has talked to me!" she said as Nancy joined her. "She tell me that she was in the library when she hear a noise. As she go into the living room to investigate, a masked man leap at her. They struggled, she break away and run upstairs toward Mrs. Alexandra's room. Just then another man step out and grab her."

"Then there must have been at least two men in the house," Nancy commented gravely. "Was Anna able to describe either of them?"

"She say both men wear black masks. Oh yes. She call the one upstairs wiry, of medium height."

"That tallies with Mrs. Alexandra's description," Nancy said thoughtfully. "I wonder if he may be one of the pickpockets the police are after."

Convinced that the clue was a vital one, Nancy waited until the nurse returned to take charge, then she went to a public telephone and called police headquarters. She reported the information received from the two patients. To her satisfaction, the desk sergeant promised that a special effort would be made to round up the long-sought pickpockets at once.

The hour was late, and Nancy knew that Hannah and her father would be worried about her. She decided to phone them, and was just about to call when Ned thrust his head into the booth.

"Keep your money if you're calling home," he advised cheerfully. "I talked to your father a while ago. He says for you to stay here as long as you're needed."

"Thanks for calling," Nancy said. "But I may as well go home. There's nothing more I can do here."

"Let's get Katherine and Jim and go somewhere to eat," Ned proposed.

"I am hungry," Nancy admitted. "We cheated ourselves out of most of the supper at the inn. But what about the party there? Shouldn't Jim go back and get Helen?"

"He phoned soon after we got here, and the party was breaking up then. Bess and Dave were going to take Helen home."

When Katherine heard this, she consented to go along, and the young people left the hospital.

"Where to?" Ned asked.

"Not many places open at this time of night," Jim replied, glancing up and down the deserted street. "I know a diner that has good food."

"Lead on!" Ned commanded. "All we ask is food and plenty of it!"

Jim escorted the party to a place that was open all night. Its only customer was a truck driver seated at the counter.

"I believe I may as well order breakfast," Nancy declared, scanning the menu. "Orange juice—"

She broke off as the door opened. A man, who was breathing hard, came hurrying in. Almost at his heels was a policeman.

"Hold on there!" the officer exclaimed, grabbing the fellow's arm. "I've got you now!"

"You've made a mistake," the man replied in a haughty voice. "Frequently I am taken for a pickpocket who closely resembles me."

"Well, we're looking for him, too."

"But my name is Dorrance."

"Doesn't mean a thing to me."

Dorrance's gaze roved about the diner and came to rest upon Nancy. His eyes brightened.

"Here's a young lady who knows me well, and knows I'm honest," he told the officer.

Smiling at Nancy, he took a handkerchief from his pocket and waved it.

"Can you identify this man?" the policeman asked her.

"Indeed I can."

Nancy arose and faced David Dorrance. "Officer, arrest this man!" she said, her words dropping like chips of steel. "He is one of the two pickpockets the police are looking for!"

CHAPTER XIX

Prisoners

David Dorrance stared at Nancy as if unable to believe his ears. He had felt certain she would exonerate him, and instead she had accused him of being wanted by the police.

"Just because I look like another man is no reason for arresting me as a thief."

"If you're innocent, you won't mind being searched," she told him.

At this remark the color drained from the man's face. The officer examined his pockets and found a large sum of money. Several bills were marked ones which had been given to a police decoy to trap the pickpockets.

"You're one of the men we're looking for, all right," the officer stated.

"You win," Dorrance said angrily. "Miss Detective, just how did you figure all this out?"

"I decided that you and your double work together. One of you picks the pocket of a victim, and either makes a quick getaway, or passes the loot to the other man through a window or a door. Then the thief plays innocent, and of course the pocketbook or wallet is never found on him.

"That handkerchief signal proved your undoing. You waved it once too often. Your pal stole a knife from Mr. Faber. In escaping, he nearly forgot to wave his handkerchief at me. Then moments later you tried the same stunt. Obviously you couldn't have moved from the office building to the store that fast."

"I didn't think you'd figure it out!" said the thief as he was led away.

Forgetting their hunger, the young people decided to follow the officer and his prisoner to police headquarters. There Nancy repeated everything she knew about the two pickpockets.

Dorrance waived his constitutional rights to consult a lawyer before answering questions. His double, he said, had stolen Mr. Drew's wallet. He admitted that both were professional pickpockets. They had met accidentally, and later worked out the partnership. When he would not tell the name of his accomplice, Nancy spoke up.

"Isn't it Cordova?"

The prisoner nodded. "I suppose that woman in the apartment house on Water Street talked," he said. "Cordova's related to her husband."

Nancy had a sudden hunch. "The husband's tall and has bushy hair, hasn't he?" she asked. "And he works with you."

Dorrance looked surprised. "That's right. He didn't want to at first, but Cordova talked him into it."

"Where is he now? At the apartment on Water Street?" Nancy asked.

"You find out!" Dorrance retorted.

"We'll round him up," the police lieutenant said quietly. "His name is Carl Peters."

In addition to the money in Dorrance's pockets, a little notebook had been found. It contained two addresses; that of a house on Clayton Avenue and the Alexandra residence.

"The Clayton Avenue place may be Cordova's hideout," said the officer. "We'll search there at once, and also the Water Street apartment. What about this Alexandra address?"

"The man arrested at the Red Lion Inn tonight lived there," Nancy explained. "I think he's associated with Dorrance, Cordova, and Peters. The four probably planned the robbery at Mrs. Alexandra's."

It was so late that Nancy and her friends did not remain longer at police headquarters. However, the next day the young detective learned by telephone that a successful raid had been staged at the Clayton Avenue house and Peters had been captured. Although Cordova escaped, all of Mrs.

Alexandra's jewels and antiques had been recovered, as well as Mr. Drew's papers.

On the way to church, she told the story to her father and Hannah Gruen. "And, Dad, you'll get back most of the money that was stolen from you!"

"That's good news." Mr. Drew sighed. "Nancy, I'm proud of the way you handled this mystery."

Later, when the family was finishing dinner, Nancy said, "As to the clue in the jewel box—well, I'm right back where I started. Prince Michael still has not been found. But I do have a good lead to work on," she added. "If he is alive, then—"

Suddenly a voice boomed through an open window. "Carson, where are you?"

The lawyer glanced at his watch. "My goodness, Nancy, that's Mr. Field. I promised to meet him twenty minutes ago. I must be off."

He kissed her affectionately, said good-by to Hannah, and left the house. Nancy immediately telephoned the hospital. She was glad to hear that Mrs. Alexandra and Anna had improved.

Next she called Katherine and learned that Richard Ellington had not contacted her.

"Oh, Nancy, I worry," the young woman said. "Richard and I are close perhaps because we are from same country. He is so kind, I do not see how he could—what you say?—break our date. He never do so before."

"I'll call his apartment," Nancy offered.

The same man who had answered the evening before said that Ellington had not come home, and had sent no word.

Deep in thought, Nancy put down the telephone. "What could have happened to Richard?"

She drove to police headquarters to obtain more information about the two prisoners. Nancy was told that the impostor prince's real name was Stanley Brandette.

"According to his story," said the lieutenant, "he met the pickpockets, Dorrance and Cordova, about two weeks ago when Cordova stole his wallet. Being a small-time thief himself, he caught on at once to the way the pickpockets' scheme worked, and told Dorrance so. Whenever Cordova was being chased after having picked someone's pocket, Dorrance would whistle in a certain way. This was a warning to drop the stolen wallet. Most pursuers would give up the chase and the thief would get away."

"The day Brandette's wallet was stolen was the first time I saw the three of them," said Nancy.

"Brandette professed admiration for the pickpockets' work, with the result that the three men became pals. Brandette had already found the prince's portfolio on the train and was planning how to rob Mrs. Alexandra."

"So the impostor wasn't keeping all the money from the sale of the jewels," said Nancy.

"No, the pickpockets were helping him dispose

of the articles and taking most of the money received for themselves. Brandette and Dorrance threatened you outside your home one night because they wanted to keep you from spoiling their scheme. Seeing that wasn't possible, they decided to loot the Alexandra home."

"Is the stolen property here?"

"Yes," replied the officer, after consulting a memorandum. "It was brought in last night. We'll have to hold everything here until Mrs. Alexandra can identify the objects."

"She may be in the hospital for several days. I was wondering—couldn't I do it for Mrs. Alexandra? Then the things could be taken to her home and put back in place."

"I think it can be arranged," the lieutenant agreed. "Can you identify the pieces?"

"A good many of them."

As Nancy went to inspect the loot she asked the officer if Brandette had volunteered any information about the real Prince Michael.

"I don't think he knows anything," the lieutenant replied. "According to Brandette's confession, he found an art portfolio left on a train seat."

"An art portfolio?" Nancy repeated meditatively.

"Yes. Discovering that the photograph and letter which it contained might lead to a fortune, Brandette decided to keep the portfolio. From the letter he knew that the name Francis Baum had been given the prince by his nurse. Evidently the woman had been afraid that if Michael Alexandra used his real name, enemies might harm him."

"Did Brandette describe the man who owned the portfolio?" Nancy asked after a moment.

"No, he refuses to give any further information."

Nancy's mind was racing. "The impostor certainly acted as if he didn't want Richard Ellington to see him that day out on the river," she thought. "Katherine did say he was from her country. Could it be possible that it was Richard's portfolio Brandette had picked up? The artist might be the lost prince!"

Nancy was brought out of her reverie by a surprising remark from the police officer.

"Brandette made an admission in regard to you. He was eavesdropping at your house and heard you discussing plans for a party at the Red Lion Inn. He made sure you saw him there so that he'd have an alibi if he was questioned about the Alexandra robbery."

"I guessed that last night. But I believe he had a second reason for appearing at the inn," Nancy said slowly. "Did he say why his companion trailed a friend of mine and me along the road?"

"I didn't know about that," the officer replied. "Brandette may do some more talking. If he does, I'll let you know."

As soon as Nancy left headquarters, she telephoned Ellington's apartment again, only to learn that no word had come from him. Later, as Nancy, Bess, and George were putting the Alexandra home in order, they discussed ways of locating the real Prince Michael, but Nancy said little.

"He must be somewhere in River Heights," Bess declared, holding a tapestry for George to tack into place on a wall.

"Nancy, you're so quiet," George commented.

"I'm worried about Richard," said Nancy. "As soon as we finish here, I propose that if he hasn't returned, we get Ned and some of the other boys and start a search for him."

"Good idea," Bess agreed.

"But shouldn't there be a police guard here when we leave?" George asked. "That thief Cordova hasn't been caught and he may come back here."

Nancy called headquarters and found out that the chief could not send a man until five o'clock, but he would stay overnight as watchman.

"That's a relief," Bess commented.

About four-thirty Katherine Kovna came to the Alexandra residence. She praised the girls' work, then asked if anyone had news of Richard Ellington. Upon receiving a negative answer and learning of another fruitless telephone call to the artist's apartment, she became excited.

"Oh, he must be in trouble!" she cried.

"A search is to be started in half an hour," said

Nancy. "The boys are going to help. Of course you'll join us?"

"Yes, yes. Where do we go?"

"To the Red Lion Inn."

"You think we may find a what-you-call 'clue' there?" Katherine asked, her face brightening.

"That's my hope. Mr. Ellington disappeared somewhere between Harbortown and the restaurant."

By the time the policeman arrived, the girls had the entire house in order, with all the returned articles in their proper places.

Katherine sighed. "If only we could find the true Prince Michael, his lovely grandmother's homecoming would be a happy one."

Immediately after a quick supper at the Red Lion Inn, the girls with Ned, Burt, Dave, and three other boys started out to hunt for Richard Ellington. Upon learning that there were two roads between Harbortown and the Red Lion Inn, they formed two searching parties. Nancy, Ned, Katherine, and Bob Dutton decided to follow the river route, while the others tried the higher road.

"It's getting dark," Ned remarked after they had walked a mile.

"I hope it doesn't rain," Nancy said as she tested her flashlight.

"Say, what's that over in those bushes?" Ned suddenly asked. "Looks like a parked car!"

They scrambled through the underbrush to examine the automobile.

"This is Richard's!" Katherine exclaimed, beside herself with worry. "What has happened?"

"There's been a struggle!" Nancy observed, beaming her light over the ground. "The grass has been trampled, and a body has been dragged along!"

Katherine murmured, "I hope no one throw Richard in river!"

The trail of trampled grass led down a steep slope to the riverbank. A short distance away stood an abandoned boathouse whose weakened posts threatened to give way beneath it. As Nancy flashed her light over it, she thought she heard a faint cry.

"Listen!" she whispered tensely.

"Help! Help!" came a weak call.

"Let's go!" Ned cried, starting forward. "Ellington may be locked in there!"

He and the girls headed for the door, but Bob took a path which led around the far side of the structure. Before they reached the water's edge, a voice boomed at them from the darkness.

"Come no closer or take the consequences!"

As the trio halted, they again heard the feeble call for help.

"What shall we do?" Katherine whispered. She was trembling.

CHAPTER XX

Two Mysteries Solved

As the weak cry for help was repeated, Ned switched on his flashlight, pointing the bright beam at the old boathouse. A man was standing on a narrow platform facing them.

"Ned! That's Cordova—the pickpocket!" Nancy whispered tensely. "Dorrance's double!"

"I'm going after him," muttered Ned, putting out his flashlight and handing it to Nancy. "When I shout, train this right in his eyes!"

"Be careful," Katherine warned anxiously.

Crouching low behind some bushes, Ned moved a little down shore. In the darkness the man on the platform could see only Nancy's light, which she was playing over the trees.

Suddenly a board creaked, there was a shout, and a flashlight was turned full on his face. The pickpocket whirled, but Ned leaped on him, and the two went down together.

Bob ran to assist. The pickpocket put up a

violent struggle, but the boys quickly subdued him.

Nancy said, "You hold him while I look inside the boathouse."

Followed by Katherine, she opened the creaking door to the old building.

"Mr. Ellington?" she called softly.

Cautiously the girls moved forward, flashing their lights over the half-rotted flooring. The water was lapping against the posts of the building.

Giant, eerie shadows leaped at them as they flashed their lights into every corner. The beam from Nancy's came to rest on an old overturned rowboat against the wall. From its stern protruded a pair of bare feet, bound with rope.

"We find someone!" Katherine cried in horror.

Nancy ran to the boat and turned it over. A glance told her that the limp figure lying on the floor was Richard Ellington. His hands were bound. A gag in his mouth had slipped a bit.

"We'll have you out of here in a second," she assured him, and worked at the knotted ropes.

Katherine already had removed the gag. "Oh, what have they done to you?" she exclaimed.

"Two masked men stopped my car," the artist said hoarsely, "and brought me here."

"Can you tell us more about them?" Nancy asked.

"Yes," the man replied. "One was tall and had

bushy hair. He called the other man Michael."

Nancy and Katherine exchanged knowing looks.

"Why did they kidnap you," Nancy asked the artist.

"I don't know," he said, puzzled.

As Nancy untied the rope that bound his ankles, she stared at Mr. Ellington's bare feet.

"Mr. Ellington! Your left foot!" she exclaimed. "It has a peculiar mark on the sole!"

"Oh, that. It was put on when I was a child. It was made by a doctor as a means of identifying me," Mr. Ellington said. "What happened in my early life is so fantastic that I never speak of it."

"Don't move," Nancy said. "I'll take this rope to my friends, so they can tie up the prisoner."

The captive was bound, then Richard Ellington was helped to his automobile. It was decided that the girls would drive him to the Red Lion Inn while the boys turned Cordova over to the police.

When they reached the inn, Nancy suggested that Katherine get a cup of hot soup for Richard Ellington. While she was gone, Nancy hurriedly asked him a few questions and was satisfied with his replies.

"Please do not tell Katherine yet," Nancy begged.

"I promise." Then he smiled and added mysteriously, "I have something special to ask her before I tell her this."

All the next day Nancy went around with a happy smile on her face and humming snatches of songs. She was planning a birthday party for her father the following evening.

"Oh, I'm glad Mrs. Alexandra will be well enough to come," she mused.

The doctor had said it would be all right for the former queen to come to the Drew home directly from the hospital. Anna would have to remain a little longer for treatment.

"I'm so happy that Mr. Faber found just the right gift for Dad!" Nancy said to Hannah Gruen.

"I am too." The housekeeper grinned. "And I'm sure your father will enjoy the party. He hasn't had a celebration in a long time."

By eight o'clock the next night all the invited guests had arrived at the Drew home. Nancy's young friends came in a group, and Mr. Ellington escorted Katherine. She proudly showed Nancy an engagement ring.

"Oh, that's wonderful!" Nancy congratulated the couple.

Mrs. Alexandra and Mr. Faber were among the last to come, the latter bearing a gift-wrapped package. Introductions were made, and Mr. Ellington's fine manners greatly impressed the former queen.

Then came the surprise of the evening. Nancy revealed that Richard Ellington was none other than the real Michael Alexandra.

She turned to Mrs. Alexandra. "He has the identifying mark on his foot."

Everyone murmured in surprise. Katherine turned white. Mrs. Alexandra gave a start, but made no sign of being pleased.

"She wants further proof," Nancy thought.

She explained that when rescuing the young man from the boathouse she had observed an A-shaped mark on his left foot.

"The incision was made by a doctor when I was a child," Mr. Ellington disclosed. "I still remember that bushy-whiskered man who made the cut."

"What else do you recall?" Mrs. Alexandra asked, still distant in her manner.

"I recall a long hallway with mirrors," Mr. Ellington said with a chuckle. "How that place frightened me!"

"It is true," whispered Mr. Faber. "He describes the Hall of Mirrors in the palace."

"Come here," Mrs. Alexandra bade the young man. "You resemble my son, but why then do you not address me in our native tongue?"

Richard Ellington laughed. Then, to the amazement of the guests, he began to speak to Mrs. Alexandra in words they could not understand. Presently she began to weep and clasped him in her arms.

Katherine, who interpreted for the group, assured them that the young man had convinced his grandmother he was the true prince. Everyone seemed to be talking at once, and Nancy was asked to explain many things.

The young detective said she had learned of the A-shaped incision from a note found in the Footman jewel box. The message had been written by Michael's nurse.

"It said that she was taking the prince to America," Nancy continued. "The faithful woman had left clues in various places, hoping his grandmother would find them upon her return to the palace.

"Only the other day Mrs. Alexandra and I discovered one of them by learning the secret of the little nightingale. The bird was made to sing the words 'clue in jewel box' by a creator of music boxes."

"That man was Conrad Nicholas, brother-in-law of my nurse, Nada," explained Mr. Ellington. Turning to his newly-found grandmother, he added, "Nada was very, very good to me. She died only six months ago, and I have been very sad since then. Not until I met Katherine did I feel happy again, but now that I have a grandmother and a fiancée, I am doubly happy."

"When did Nada write that letter which the impostor used?" George asked.

"She wrote it when I was still a little boy. Nada wanted me to have proof of my identity in case anything happened to her," the artist replied.

"She gave me the name Francis Baum so our enemies would not find us. Later I took the name Richard Ellington."

"I like that much better," said his grandmother. "And I do not mind if you keep using it. I shall never call you Michael, for it will bring up memories of that awful thief."

"He's a kidnapper, too," said Nancy. She explained that he had confessed kidnapping Richard Ellington to keep Nancy and her friends busy searching for him. "With us out of the way he hoped we wouldn't have time to investigate the robbery when it was revealed."

The true prince spoke up. "After I lost my art portfolio on the train, I often wondered what became of my toy lamb. Nada warned me to keep it as extra proof of my identity. I was embarrassed to let anyone see it in my room, so I kept it in my portfolio."

"It is waiting for you at your new home." Mrs. Alexandra smiled gaily. "That is, if you will live with me until your marriage."

After the thrilling reunion, still another surprise awaited the guests. Nancy arose, kissed her father, and said, "Happy Birthday, Dad! For a special reason I am asking Mr. Faber to present my gift."

The antique dealer stood up. In a ceremonious speech he declared that it gave him great pleasure to present the gentleman's box.

"It will now be in the home of the finest, most unselfish people I have ever met—Mr. Drew and his lovely, clever daughter!"

There was much handclapping as Nancy and her father acknowledged the compliment. Everyone crowded close as the package was unwrapped. Mr. Drew lifted out a handsome leather and silver box, its lid embossed with a scene of hunters on horseback. It bore the mark of the skilled silversmith who had created it—Mr. Faber's father.

"This is very fine and most unique," Mr. Drew declared, his fingers exploring the intricate work.

Suddenly he gasped in astonishment. Somehow the lawyer had pressed a tiny, hidden spring along the side of the gentleman's box. A false bottom was revealed, and in it was a slip of paper.

"Now what can this be?" Mr. Drew asked as he scanned the strange figures on the sheet.

"Until this moment I did not know that the box had a secret opening," put in Mr. Faber.

"Hm! A formula of some sort," Mr. Drew said.

"Perhaps the long-missing process of enamel making!" exclaimed Mr. Faber. "At one time my father had it in his possession."

Mr. Drew offered the paper to the man, saying, "Then this belongs to you."

Mr. Faber retreated a step. "No! No! It is yours too. I can take back nothing."

Mr. Drew turned to his daughter. "What do

you think, dear? After all, you are the one who solved this whole mystery."

Nancy locked arms with her father. "I think you should remain a lawyer and I an amateur detective. The formula is Mr. Faber's."

Everyone applauded this idea. Now that the mystery had come to a close, Nancy began to wonder when and where her next adventure would take place. It proved to be an exciting one, called *The Secret in the Old Attic.*

Mr. Faber had started to speak. "Any profit I make I want to share with all of you. My gift will include a large donation to the Boys Club and a wedding present to the prince and his bride."

Mrs. Alexandra smiled at everyone. "I sincerely hope for continued friendship among us all, and I give especially warm thanks for my great happiness and good fortune to our darling Nancy Drew."

DETACH ALONG DOTTED LINE AND MAIL IN ENVELOPE WITH PAYMENT

ORDER FORM

NANCY DREW MYSTERY SERIES

Now that you've met Nancy Drew and her friends, we're sure you'll want to "accompany" them on other exciting adventures. So for your convenience, we've enclosed this handy order form.

54 TITLES AT YOUR BOOKSELLER OR COMPLETE AND MAIL THIS HANDY COUPON TO:

GROSSET & DUNLAP, INC.
P.O. Box 941, Madison Square Post Office, New York, N.Y. 10010

Please send me the Nancy Drew Mystery Book(s) checked below @ $2.50 each, plus 25¢ *per book* postage and handling. My check or money order for $________ is enclosed.

	Title	No.
☐	1. Secret of the Old Clock	9501-7
☐	2. Hidden Staircase	9502-5
☐	3. Bungalow Mystery	9503-3
☐	4. Mystery at Lilac Inn	9504-1
☐	5. Secret of Shadow Ranch	9505-X
☐	6. Secret of Red Gate Farm	9506-8
☐	7. Clue in the Diary	9507-6
☐	8. Nancy's Mysterious Letter	9508-4
☐	9. The Sign of the Twisted Candles	9509-2
☐	10. Password to Larkspur Lane	9510-6
☐	11. Clue of the Broken Locket	9511-4
☐	12. The Message in the Hollow Oak	9512-2
☐	13. Mystery of the Ivory Charm	9513-0
☐	14. The Whispering Statue	9514-9
☐	15. Haunted Bridge	9515-7
☐	16. Clue of the Tapping Heels	9516-5
☐	17. Mystery of the Brass Bound Trunk	9517-3
☐	18. Mystery at Moss-Covered Mansion	9518-1
☐	19. Quest of the Missing Map	9519-X
☐	20. Clue in the Jewel Box	9520-3
☐	21. The Secret in the Old Attic	9521-1
☐	22. Clue in the Crumbling Wall	9522-X
☐	23. Mystery of the Tolling Bell	9523-8
☐	24. Clue in the Old Album	9524-6
☐	25. Ghost of Blackwood Hall	9525-4
☐	26. Clue of the Leaning Chimney	9526-2
☐	27. Secret of the Wooden Lady	9527-0
☐	28. The Clue of the Black Keys	9528-9
☐	29. Mystery at the Ski Jump	9529-7
☐	30. Clue of the Velvet Mask	9530-0
☐	31. Ringmaster's Secret	9531-9
☐	32. Scarlet Slipper Mystery	9532-7
☐	33. Witch Tree Symbol	9533-5
☐	34. Hidden Window Mystery	9534-3
☐	35. Haunted Showboat	9535-1
☐	36. Secret of the Golden Pavilion	9536-X
☐	37. Clue in the Old Stagecoach	9537-8
☐	38. Mystery of the Fire Dragon	9538-6
☐	39. Clue of the Dancing Puppet	9539-4
☐	40. Moonstone Castle Mystery	9540-8
☐	41. Clue of the Whistling Bagpipes	9541-6
☐	42. Phantom of Pine Hill	9542-4
☐	43. Mystery of the 99 Steps	9543-2
☐	44. Clue in the Crossword Cipher	9544-0
☐	45. Spider Sapphire Mystery	9545-9
☐	46. The Invisible Intruder	9546-7
☐	47. The Mysterious Mannequin	9547-5
☐	48. The Crooked Banister	9548-3
☐	49. The Secret of Mirror Bay	9549-1
☐	50. The Double Jinx Mystery	9550-5
☐	51. Mystery of the Glowing Eye	9551-3
☐	52. The Secret of the Forgotten City	9552-1
☐	53. The Sky Phantom	9553-X
☐	54. The Strange Message in the Parchment	9554-1

SHIP TO:

NAME ____
(please print)

ADDRESS ____

CITY ____________________ STATE ____________________ ZIP ____________________